WHY DON'T YOU STAY? ... FOREVER

McLaughlin Brothers, Book 2

JENNIFER ASHLEY

JA / AG Publishing

Chapter One

Ben

"BEN, I AM *SO* SORRY!" Erin has removed her glasses, and her beautiful eyes are wide with horror.

"I'm all right ..." I wheeze, gasping for air, black dots spinning before me.

It's not every day you're kicked in the privates by the woman of your dreams. I mean that literally—her foot smacks right into my crotch.

It's not Erin's fault—the blame is all on me.

Here's what happened: I work at my family's business as the IT guy, because none of my brothers, or my mom or dad, really understands computers. I mean, even the most basic stuff. Kinda sad, though I don't mind helping out.

I like to take a stroll at lunch and get out of my cave —as my brothers call my office where the servers are. Today, in the middle of May, it's stifling hot, about a hundred in the shade, so I duck back inside early. In Phoenix, air conditioning is our friend.

Our office is a showroom where we display a few high-tech kitchens and bathrooms, and where we meet with clients, show them sample books, etcetera etcetera. At least, Austin, Zach, or Ryan meet them and schmooze, while I make sure the tech works so my brothers can process the orders and we get paid.

Around the small showroom are a ring of offices, and a high-counter reception desk just inside the front door.

The reception desk is empty as I clomp back inside. I feel a twinge of disappointment—I'd hoped Erin Dixon, the temp since our previous secretary retired, would be there. I could casually lean on the desk and say hi.

Erin is gorgeous. Long, sleek brown hair, big blue eyes behind glasses. She has a dancer's body, because she's an actual dancer. She's with the West Valley Ballet, apparently a well-respected company, not that I know much about ballet.

I head to the break room. That's set up with a table and chairs, a few vending machines, a microwave, and a big fridge, so any of us can eat lunch here if we want. Mostly my brothers go out or home, but I usually eat in my office and then take a walk.

Halfway to the break room I hear music.

Not the raunchy, dance club stuff Austin listens to, or the popular music Zach likes. It's rippling piano music I'm unfamiliar with, lilting and magical.

Through the window next to the break room's door, I see Erin.

She's dancing. She's donned a tank top and bicycle shorts, and she's bending and stretching, her limbs in graceful arcs.

I've never seen anything more beautiful in my life.

I halt, stunned, and watch her. She rests one hand lightly on the back of a chair, while she lifts a leg into the air, swiftly, precisely. Down it goes, then up again, liquid high kicks.

Erin drops her head back, eyes closed, one arm curved above her. Her chin juts out in a regal pose, like a sculpture. I'm frozen in place by the beauty of it—the human body at its most amazing.

I realize I can't stand out here ogling her like a peeping Tom. I open the door noisily to alert her, but any sound is drowned by the music streaming from her phone.

Up goes her leg again, and she bounces high on the ball of her other foot.

"Hey, Erin. Sorry to—"

She pirouettes to the music, her leg sweeping around. She sees me at the last minute and tries to stop, but the momentum carries her, and her outstretched foot slams right into my crotch.

"Oh, shit. *Ben* ..."

I double over in serious pain, which recedes slightly when I feel her slender, cool fingers on my arm.

"Ben—you okay?"

The music plunges on, the piano's chords crashing

through the room. Erin lunges away and silence falls, except for her ragged breathing and my groans.

"Ben, I am *so* sorry." Erin's face comes into view. "Here, sit down."

"I'm all right." The words are barely audible, escaping from my mouth like air leaking from a tire.

I drop into the chair, trying not to grab myself down below. The poor guys are aching, but the rest of me tingles with awareness. Erin smells good, like the golden flowers that burst into bloom around here every spring.

"Can I get you anything?" she's asking. "I didn't see you. I didn't mean ..."

"Erin." I rest my hand on hers, the smoothness of her skin starting to ease the pain. "It's okay. I shouldn't have sneaked up on you."

"I had the music on too loud. I thought everyone was gone. I'm trying to practice—I'm an understudy and I have to take over the lead on Saturday night. I'm so nervous, and I figured I might as well use the time to ..."

"Hey." Boldly I lift my fingers and rest them over her mouth as she babbles. "I said it's okay."

We both freeze. Her breath is warm on my fingers, and my extremities start recovering enough to react.

Erin takes a quick step back, her face beet red. I'm torn between sitting in misery or reaching for her again.

But the last thing I want is her running to the head of HR and saying I engaged in inappropriate touching. Especially since the head of HR is my mom.

Erin stars gathering up her stuff—phone, gym bag, paper wrapping that once held her lunch. Her movements are jerky and quick, the complete opposite of the grace that flowed in her dance.

"Are *you* okay?" I ask. "You whacked me pretty good. Did you hurt your foot?"

Erin sticks it out, her legs bare from the shins down, soft ballet slippers cupping her feet. She rotates the foot in question, flexing it and her ankle.

"Fine I think. I'll just go back to work."

"Hang on a sec." I climb to my feet, my balls still throbbing, but the ache is lessening. She'd pulled her kick at the last minute, which made me not want to think about how I'd feel right now if she hadn't.

Erin tosses out her trash. "I'm really, really sorry, Ben. I shouldn't have been using the break room for my personal time ..."

"Why not? Everyone else does. Austin brought friends in here to sing karaoke one night. Long time ago. He still hasn't lived it down."

"I'm just ... I don't want to lose this job ..."

I step in front of her as she tries to hightail it out the door. I've been thrown together with this woman for weeks now, as I'm the only one who can train her in our tech and software systems. When she has a problem, she comes straight to me.

I love being her geek-in-shining armor, but we never talk about anything other than how to use the new software I've been working on. Not real talking, as in I want to know everything about her.

"You think I'll ask Mom to fire you because you kicked me in the nuts?" I grin to myself as I picture the look on my mother's face. "She'd make it all my fault anyway. She likes you."

Erin's mouth droops. "I feel terrible."

I can't take Erin's sad eyes as she snatches up her glasses and shoves them on. I want to put my arms around her and comfort her. Maybe hold on a while longer, for more than comfort.

"It was a stupid accident. I'm fine. Really." I gyrate my hips to show her, hoping to make her laugh.

I'm rewarded with a faint smile, and I reflect that this is the most natural conversation we've ever had. Mostly I can barely open my mouth except for IT talk, and she says, *Yes, Sure, I understand,* and *Thank you.*

Erin wets her lips, which zings my attention straight to them. Full, sweet, red lips ... "Tell you what," she's saying. "Would you like to come to the performance Saturday night? I can give you some tickets ... Unless, well, it's ballet, and not everyone's interest—"

"Sounds great. Thanks." I dive into her flow of words. Would I like to sit and watch Erin in a leotard, or whatever they're called, float around a stage, moving her body in ways that will make my dreams seriously interesting? Hell yes.

"Really?" Erin's surprise is amusing.

"Really." Yes, the IT guy with the Star Wars poster and signed photo with Levar Burton in his cubicle is interested in watching ballet. At least ballet with Erin in it.

"Great. I'll get it fixed up." She hesitates. "Would your brothers like to come? Or your parents?"

"My brothers? I doubt it." I shake my head. "Ryan and Calandra are busy being newlyweds, and Abby and Zach are getting ready to be. Notice how both those couples went home for lunch?"

Erin's sudden smile is like sunshine. "I know. They think they're being discreet. It's adorable."

Aw, she thinks my brothers and the loves of their lives are adorable. That bodes well.

"And Austin—he's just ... busy."

I have no idea what Austin will be up to Saturday night, and I don't care. I just know I won't want him there.

"Your mom and dad?"

"I'll ask them." I really want this to be just Erin and me, but I need to be polite. She's inviting me because she's trying to make things up to me, not because she thinks I'm hot. Plus, Mom is interested in Erin's dancing and would probably love to go.

"Good." Erin gives me another warm look that dissipates all pain I've ever felt. "I'll make a call."

Her smile turns shy, and she darts a glance past me. I realize I'm blocking the door, as though I'll keep her in here, speaking stiltedly with me all afternoon. Which wouldn't be a bad thing, but again, she might complain to HR, and Mom will be all over my case.

I step aside and Erin slides past me, almost running on her light feet. Hard to believe such an elegant, gorgeous woman can kick like a mule. The immediate pain is fading, but I'm going to be sore for a while.

I don't mind. Erin can kick me all she wants if she smiles at me like that for the rest of her life.

————

Erin

BEN IS HERE. I PEER AT HIM THROUGH THE BREAK in the curtain that separates our stage from the small house. Our company has taken over a historic theater in old-town Glendale not far from the library. True, the occasional freight train rumbles through along Grand and shakes the building to its foundations, but it has thick brick walls, and the orchestra usually drowns out the noise.

Ben occupies the seat I'd reserved for him—second row, almost in the middle. First row is filled with friends of the theater's owner and major sponsors. In my opinion, the second row has a better view anyway.

He's come alone. I hadn't heard whether Virginia and Alan, Ben's parents who own McLaughlin Renovations, could make it, but I'd reserved three seats. Ben has taken the end one, but he must have either given away or turned in the other two tickets, because strangers, a senior couple, sit beside him. This will make Clarice, who owns our company, happy—she doesn't like empty seats.

Ben—the   fine-looking,   low-voiced,   genius

McLaughlin brother who is sweeter than any man has a right to be—idly glances through his program. He's dressed up, for Ben, wearing a collared shirt and a tie. I wonder if he's paired that with jeans and wish he'd stand up so I can find out. Plus I could admire his nice, tight ass.

Ben will be watching me dance. I get a sudden case of the shakes.

"Easy there." Dean, the principal male dancer, squeezes my elbow and leans to whisper into my ear. "Don't get nervous, sweetie. I might drop you."

He flashes white teeth in amusement. Dean is a hell of a dancer, and never makes mistakes. I'll be dancing several *pas de deuxes* with him as the stand-in for the female principal, Julia, who unhappily broke her leg in several places in a freak fall off her own porch steps.

"Please don't," I beg him. "Clarice will never let me hear the end of it."

"Aw, I'd take the blame. But really, what's up? You've been steady as a rock all week. No reason to be nervous. You'll be awesome."

There's a reason everyone likes Dean. You'd think as lead dancer he'd be a total arrogant shit, but he is supportive, encouraging, and just a nice guy.

"First night jitters?" I offer. "I don't want to make you look bad."

"Right. Oh." Dean catches the direction of my gaze through the crack in the curtain. "Aha. First night jitters, my ass. New boyfriend?"

"No." My answer snaps out before I can stop it. "He works at my office. I offered tickets to everyone there, but he was the only one who could make it." Sounds like a reasonable explanation.

"Uh-huh. Your rosy cheeks are from more than makeup, sweetie. You have the hots for him?"

"The hots?" I give him an incredulous look, but my face grows warm even as I deny the truth. "What are we, twelve?"

"No, we're all grown up, which makes it much better. Don't worry, honey." Dean gently rubs my shoulders. "You'll wow him."

"I seriously wish I had your confidence."

"It's not confidence. It's practice. I practice, you practice. We know this. We'll do it."

He gives my shoulders a pat and strides off to spew his pep talks on the other dancers who wait nervously for the performance to begin.

The orchestra in the pit ceases their warmup and quiets. For a moment, all is silence, then the conductor's baton comes down and music slams into the theater. My heart lurches with it. The audience applauds in anticipation then begins to subside, the rousing overture covering the sound of rustling programs.

This ballet isn't a classical one—Clarice, the company manager and chief choreographer, writes her own shows. It's a modern composition that employs mostly classical moves with some modern dancing. Clarice is very good, so even people who prefer the tried-and-true ballets like *Giselle*, *Swan Lake*, or *The Nutcracker*, usually like her offerings. We always have a full house.

As the overture ends, the *corps de ballet*—a group containing most of the company—flutters on and goes through a lovely dance, which I'd been in before Julia got injured. Now I wait in the wings to go on as a principal.

I always considered the opening dance long, but tonight, it seems *very* short. Soon the dancers are rushing off, transforming from ethereal creatures to panting, sweating human beings as they run from the stage, and finally it's my turn.

I'm on.

Alone.

In front of Ben McLaughlin, an amazing man I've had a crush on since the first moment I met him.

Chapter Two

Ben

IT'S safe to say I don't know shit about dancing. But when Erin enters the stage in a series of gliding leaps, her long legs reaching, it doesn't matter.

People around me applaud in admiration. I can't bring up my hands to join in, because I'm stunned.

Erin, the woman I can watch clicking a mouse all day, has been transformed. Her glasses are gone, her long hair slicked back from her face into a bun held by a glittery net. Her stage makeup makes her eyes pop, and her lips are a kissable red.

She's wearing a skin-tight, allover thing that bares her arms and lower legs. The costume looks tie-dyed in light colors, reds and yellows. It draws attention to the elegant lines of her body, no tutus or whatever to distract from the beauty of her.

As I say, I don't know shit about dancing. I don't know the names of the moves Erin makes as her arms sculpt the air and her legs scissor-kick. Her jumps put her in midair for a split second, before she lands softly on her ballet shoes. No what-do-you-call-them—toe shoes—just regular slippers.

She rises high on her right toe, her left leg going straight up, then she pivots in the move I recognize. The one that slammed her foot into my groin.

I chuckle, which earns me a stern frown from the lady in front of me. I choke off, hoping Erin didn't hear me.

I see a little twinkle in her eyes as she comes out of it and looks right at me. I grin back.

She spins abruptly away, moving faster and faster, her arms coming up like an ice skater's as she twirls.

Erin finishes her pirouettes at the far end of the stage, then comes running back, does a few more spins in place, and ends everything in a low, leg-extended bow.

The crowd goes wild and applauds like crazy. I'm joining in, my palms tingling, and I hear, *Bravo!* escape my mouth.

What the fuck? I've never said anything like that in my life. I sound like Jean-Luc Picard.

But it's appropriate. Erin is incredible. I do a fist-pump for her, which earns me another frown from Mrs. Hoity-Toity in the first row.

The applause only dies down when the orchestra starts up again. Now a guy comes tearing out from the wings. Erin retreats to the back of the stage, standing in a quiet pose while the guy leaps around. He pretty much flies. If ballet were an Olympic sport, he'd be ranking perfect 10s.

Erin lets him have his glory. The crowd loves him, clapping at every move he makes. I find myself doing it too, because I'm impressed.

Finally, he ends his dance by twirling in the air a few times and landing on strong feet. The cheers swamp him.

Then he turns around and spies Erin. His face crumples as though Cupid's arrow has just shot through him. He runs joyfully to her and pulls her into a dance.

I enjoy it at first—two talented people showing off what they can do. But I start to not like this guy's hands all over Erin. I tell myself it's nothing—he has to lift her in the air and assist in her gravity defying moves. When I was a little kid, Ryan, a pre-teen then, used to put his hands under my chest and thighs and raise me high, and I'd pretend I was flying. The male dancer—Dean Whitaker, the program says his name is—does much the same thing with Erin.

But I'm hoping he's not having too much fun up there.

Erin and Dean move together fluidly, her smaller frame inside his big body. Her kicks avoid his groin entirely.

Their grace makes me feel large and clumsy.

Maybe I should have learned dance when I was younger instead of hunkering down to master C++.

The dance ends to thunderous applause. I'm on my feet too, because even I realize they are really, really good.

The show goes on. There are more dance numbers, and a loose story that goes with it, according to the program, all about the seasons, with a nod toward global warming and Venus—the planet, not the goddess. Against it are two people falling in love or at least dancing and looking at each other like they're hurting inside.

The final dance between Erin and Dean is quiet and full of sensual moves. Erin flows with him. After a while, I forget about being envious of the man and look only at her.

Erin is beauty itself. I bask in her, every move she makes precise and effortless. I swell with pride—that's my girl, the one who's so quick to catch on to our company's software's little quirks. Far faster than my brothers have ever done. Austin still can't work his damned computer.

Before I realize it, Erin and Dean twirl around each other and come to a halt in a curved stance, the two of them like a Renaissance statue. Applause thunders.

Erin and Dean rise out of their final pose and make their bows. Dean presents Erin with a sweep of his arm, breaking character to clap for her as Erin does her low curtsy.

Bouquets of flowers flow toward the stage, which

Erin accepts with a happy but humble smile. Now I feel like a jerk because I didn't bring her any. I didn't realize it was a thing. I guess I'll know better next time.

The thought jolts me. Will there be a next time? Or is this a one-off? Erin gave me the tickets to apologize for kicking the hell out of me. Trying to save her job. Would she want me here again?

I vow right then there'll be a next time. I'll buy my own ticket and give Erin so many flowers she won't be able to walk off the stage with them.

Like now. Dean helps her, laughing and pleased at all the attention she's getting. He bows to her too, and pats her on the back like, "Well done, you!"

The lights come up and the curtain rings down. The audience starts drifting out, talking excitedly. They say great things about Erin—who knew she was so talented?

"What was her name?" the lady who'd been sitting next to me says. She had been on stand-by to see the show, able to come in because I'd turned in the other two tickets Erin had given me. I hadn't said anything, but she'd been so pleased she and her husband had been able to get in. "She was wonderful."

"Erin Dixon," I tell her proudly. "She's a friend." I think I'm glowing.

"Well, she did great tonight," the lady says, patting my arm. "Tell her that when you go backstage to see her."

Another jolt. I can go backstage to see her? I

abruptly want to—want it more than anything else. I can't leave until I do.

I say good-night to my seat mate, head down the aisle to the stage, and start arguing with the security guard, who takes up a stern stance and forbids me going past him and behind the curtain.

————

Erin

"Hey, sweetie, I think your new guy is trying to find you."

Dean, who is surrounded by his admirers, mostly women, shoots me a wink and points through the gap in the curtain. I see one of the theater's security guards trying to send Ben away.

I push the curtain aside and hurry to the front. "It's all right," I tell the guard. "He's with me."

Ben and the security guy break off their harried debate. The security guard flicks a hand in resignation, and I gesture Ben up the steps on the side of the stage.

"Thanks so much for being here," I say as Ben climbs the stairs. "Come and meet everyone."

I'm breathing hard, even more than I had been during the last *pas de deux*. A couple of those moves were tough, and Dean and I had practiced them until we couldn't move.

Ben glances around with interest as I lead him backstage. "I didn't bring you flowers, sorry."

"Oh, that's okay. Some people follow the tradition. Plus, this was for my opening night. I'm so grateful people liked it. We usually donate them to retirement homes—I couldn't take them all home with me."

I'm babbling nervously, but Ben does that to me. He's the smartest man I've ever met, and I'm always afraid of being a dunce in front of him.

"You were good," Ben says, true admiration in his eyes.

My face gets hot. I bet my makeup is running, and I look like a raccoon. "Thank you. I was seriously nervous."

"It didn't show. You seemed perfectly calm. The lady sitting next to me said to tell you that you were awesome. Okay, she didn't say *awesome*. But it's what she meant."

"You are so sweet."

Ben's eyes flicker, and I want to bite my tongue. No guy wants to be told he's sweet.

"Hello." Dean's deep voice booms out behind me. "I'm Dean. I hear you're Ben. Great to meet you. Wasn't Erin fantastic?"

Dean and Ben are about the same height, but the likeness ends there. Dean's face is painted with bright makeup, his muscles bulge out of his leotard, and he exudes charm. A girl is supposed to fall for guys like Dean.

Ben to me is far more appealing. He's in great shape—I've seen him in shorts and T-shirt at backyard cookouts at his parents' house. He looks *very* good in them. Ben carries himself casually, as though he doesn't realize how attractive he is. He considers himself a nerd next to his jock brothers, but he's as agile and athletic as they are.

Dean beams at Ben, shaking his hand hard.

"Erin was fantastic." Ben's words make me hot all over. "Oh, you were good too," he adds hastily to Dean.

Dean roars with laughter. "I know where your eyes were. I can't blame you, bud. You two kids take care."

He pivots, still laughing, and returns to his fans.

Ben's brow wrinkles as though he's worried he offended Dean, then he laughs. I've never heard him laugh. It's warm and nice. "I like him."

"Most people do. Dean's one of a kind. Um." I stop myself shuffling my feet as I return to the self-consciousness I feel in front of Ben. "I need to change and scrape off this makeup. Want to come with me to get food after?"

"Sure." The answer is instant. "This isn't the best neighborhood anyway. I planned to walk you to your car."

I tamp down my joy with difficulty. "My car's not here. I rode with Ida—one of the other dancers."

"Oh." Ben sounds disappointed. He rubs his upper lip. "Is this food-getting a thing you all do together?"

"Yes. Another tradition. But ... afterward. Would you drive me home? Unless—if it's out of your way, then don't worry about it—"

"Sure." Again Ben's word cuts over my fumbling

ones. "How about you go get changed, and I'll take you to your party?"

"Good." I grab both his hands. "Stay right here."

I run off to the dressing rooms, ready to tear off my costume and rush out again, my feet lighter than they'd been the entire performance.

————

Ben

DURING THE DRIVE TO A BURGER BAR THAT'S actually open past ten on a Saturday night—a rarity in this town—I find my tongue leaden and my conversation stilted. My brain comes up with witty things to say to Erin, and I can't utter a one of them.

Erin's excited and bouncy, coming out of the quiet shell she keeps herself in at work. Of course, compared to my obnoxious brothers, anyone seems quiet, but tonight she's sparkling.

She stretches her bare legs under shorts in my roomy pickup, sneakers pointing. "Dang, my feet hurt." Her laugh sounds like music. "No duh, right? Keeping up with Dean is rough."

"You, uh." I clear my throat. I have to ask before I get too optimistic. "Anything between you and Dean?"

Erin shoots me wide-eyed surprise. "Dean? Not at all. I'm not his type, and he's not mine."

"Ah." I run that through my brain. "Is he gay?" It's

the only reason I can think of for a man not to be interested in Erin. I try not to sound hopeful.

"He's bi." Erin answers without hesitation. "Everyone knows that—he came out in his teens. He calls himself a 'people person'."

I burst out laughing, willing my jealousy to recede. "He's kinda cool. Not what I expected."

"Everyone likes Dean."

She says it neutrally, no big deal. I guess if I was built like the Hulk but could dance like I was in zero gravity, everyone would like me too.

We trail off into silence. Erin starts to hum as we pass street after street, traffic light after traffic light. In Phoenix, no two places you want to go in one night are ever close together.

I pull into the burger bar, the parking lot full. The late-night grubbers know where the few after-hours restaurants in the Valley are. I wouldn't be surprised to find Austin, the night owl, here.

Takes me a while, but I finally locate a parking space at the edge of the lot. I try to get around the truck to usher Erin out, but she agilely leaps down before I can. She doesn't notice my disappointment as we make for the restaurant.

Inside it's packed. The dance company has reserved a back room, and that's packed too. Dean is holding court, surrounded by people who hang on his every word. The rest of the dancers are in clumps with friends and family, everyone laughing and talking.

I'm uncomfortable, because I don't know anyone.

This shy guy has no business walking into a room full of strangers.

Erin sticks by me as we squeeze through. She introduces me to her fellow dancers, men and women, who give me interested stares.

"I work with Ben at my temp job," she explains. "I whacked him good while I was rehearsing and had to make it up to him."

Everyone she tells this story to finds it hilarious. They seem to like Erin, exhibiting no jealousy that she got to dance the lead role with the fabulous Dean. At least, if they are envious, they hide it well.

Erin finds us a table in the mob, and I flag down the waitress working the room. We order burgers. When they arrive, Erin doesn't pick at hers. She downs it, wiping grease from her mouth with a wad of paper napkins.

"I earned this."

"You did." I want to tell her how amazing she was, how wonderful a dancer, how much I loved watching her. But the room is loud, and I'd have to scream it at her. I settle for eating my burger and fries, the two of us sharing the occasional smile.

Dean, who has more stamina than anyone really should, starts a drinking game. Since the game consists of balancing a bottle or mug of beer on the head while doing a dance move, I stay out of it. Some of the company is good at it—I suspect they've played it before.

Erin watches for a while, sipping iced tea. She

glances at me. "Want to get out of here?" she asks in my ear.

I shrug like I don't care, but my heart is racing. I try to signal the waitress to pay the tab, but Erin forestalls me. The manager, Clarice, has picked up the bill for the company and guests.

"Nice of her," I say.

"She's generous." Erin presses close to me as we slide out of the room. "This company is her baby and she does all she can for it. We're lucky."

I respond in the affirmative, and then we're out in the parking lot, the darkness comforting. It's cooled down a little from the heat of the May day, the breeze refreshing.

Erin steps from me as soon as we're out of the crowd, but I move closer again. This time I manage to open the pickup's door for her, and she gives me a thank-you glance as she leaps gracefully inside.

I jog around to the driver's door and, far more ungainly, get myself into the seat. I start the truck.

"Where to?"

She gives me a startled look. "Did you want to go somewhere else?"

"No—I said I'd drive you home, but I don't know where you live."

"Oh." She flushes. "It's not far from the office actually. Twelfth Street and Glendale. I have a house behind there."

"Got it."

Fifteen minutes later, I turn off Glendale and

follow her directions to halt in front of a small place with a well-kept yard. This is an older neighborhood but one that has seen a turnaround in the last twenty years. Our company has worked on some of the houses here.

Once away from Phoenix's major streets, the neighborhoods can be quiet and homey. Erin's house has been remodeled, it looks like, with a glass block wall near her front door.

Her house. Where she lives, sleeps, undresses ...

Damn it, why the hell did I have to think of that?

I'm now imagining Erin gracefully sliding her clothes from her body and dropping them on the floor. Her bare skin comes into view. My view only. She's undressing for *me*.

"Well, thanks for coming," Erin says, breaking my treacherous thoughts. "And for driving me home. I hope you liked the performance."

"Yeah. It was nice."

Nice. Oh, good one. I'm again blowing my chance to tell her how wonderful she was, but I don't have the words to describe it. Three hours from now, I will, I'm sure, when I'm lying alone in my bed, aching, unable to think about anything but her.

On impulse, I move abruptly toward Erin, turn her to me, and kiss her parted lips.

One touch, her lips smooth, her breath warming mine. My body goes molten, melting like silicon into glass.

I pull back. *Shit.* I just kissed her. I wait for her to

smack me or snarl at me, or worse, threaten to tell my mom.

Erin watches me a moment, her eyes glistening in the dashboard light. I start to turn away, give her the chance to get out and run, when she grabs me by the shirt, hauls me across the center column, and kisses the hell out of me.

Chapter Three

Erin

I EXPECT Ben to tear himself away and shove me out of the truck, but he pulls me closer, gentling the hard kiss I'd hammered him with.

Fire washes me as he caresses my mouth, his tongue sliding inside. My fingers sink into his shirt, finding hard muscle beneath.

His lips are strong, the burn of unshaved whiskers on my skin. Ben cups my head, holding me steady. I'm shaking all over and feel safe at the same time.

I want to kiss him forever, but it's not practical, so we ease apart. He hovers near me, his gaze on my lips, his fingers brushing my cheek.

"I've been wanting to do that since I met you," he says in a quiet voice.

I swallow. "Yeah? The nerdy girl with glasses?"

"The beautiful woman with amazing eyes. *I'm* the nerd in this equation."

"That's a matter of opinion," I say shakily.

"That's right. My opinion."

I make a noise that sounds like a giggle. Seriously, I haven't giggled since I was a little kid. But then, I've never met a guy who makes me feel like Ben does—silly, young, excited ...

"Want to come in?" I say it casually. No pressure. This doesn't have to lead to sex. We can just talk. Right?

Ben hesitates. Any second, he'll say, *I really should be going,* and I'll nod, understanding. No pressure, remember?

"Sure," he says.

Ben kills the engine and opens his door. I sit there like a fool until he's halfway around the truck. I realize he means it—he's going to accompany me inside.

I open the door and leap out. As he had at the restaurant, he looks a bit let down, and I realize he wanted to do the gentlemanly thing of opening my door. He really is sweet.

Ben locks up his truck, and I fumble for my keys to the front door. I find them, drop them, and dive for the ground, groping in the dark. Of course they've landed in the gravel beyond the doorstep, outside the circle of the porch light.

Ben crouches down, helping me look. Our hands touch, and I let out that stupid giggly sound again. Please, make me stop.

"Careful," I tell Ben. "There's a cactus ..."

He yelps as the words come out of my mouth. I have desert landscaping in my small yard—saves water and it's easy to take care of, as I'm rarely home.

Ben jerks his arm up. My keys dangle from his hand, and so do spines from the prickly pear he's shoved them into. He shakes his hand, keys jangling, but I know from experience the spines won't be dislodged so easily.

I grab the keys and open the door, waving him inside. I slam the door closed and drop my keys onto a table, hitting the light switch before Ben can fall over the furniture in my tiny house.

I take him by the arm and pull him down the hall past my bedroom to the bathroom. "Sorry," I say.

"I'm the idiot who stuck his hand in a cactus," Ben rumbles.

I have the water running in the sink, the antiseptic out of the medicine cabinet, and duct tape from the cabinet on the wall. When I redid the bathroom two years ago, I went with a retro feel, installing a sink with legs, a clawfoot tub, and black and white tile on the floor.

To Ben, whose family renovates lavish homes in the town of Paradise Valley—the swank stretch that runs from Camelback Mountain north to Shea—it probably looks dorky, but I did it myself with finds from big box stores and the Park and Swap. I had a plumbing party and my dance friends helped out. I was expunging my life of another person, and they knew it.

I know how to get cactus thorns out of flesh, because I've had the problem before. Prickly pear can be nasty, driving dozens of tiny needles into the skin. Fortunately Ben hasn't gotten a big dose. I pour water and antiseptic on his hand, pat his skin carefully dry with a towel, and then unroll the duct tape.

"Seriously?"

"Works like a dream." I gingerly lay the tape across the back of his hand, where the needles stand up, then lightly tap it down. "Ready?"

"No." Ben gives me a wavering smile. "But what the hell?"

I grasp the tape, and yank. He grunts with pain. The spines come out—most of them anyway. I triumphantly fold up the tape several times and drop it into the trash.

We're not done yet. I take up the tweezers, bend over his hand and start to gently work out the half dozen spines still in his skin.

"This is the weirdest date I've ever been on," Ben says, his breath ruffling my hair.

A date? Is that what this is? My heart thumps, and I try to quiet it. No, he's joking. Right?

"Me too." I drop each spine down the sink. Ben's hand is red from the duct tape, but there's not much bleeding. "Not that I go on many. Too busy."

"Dancing takes up a lot of time?"

"Only if you want to be good at it."

I concentrate on the spines and the tweezers. I don't

want to talk about my failed love life with Reuben, a dancer who is almost as good as Dean but without the winning personality. Which I discovered too late.

Reuben is why I remodeled the bathroom and the rest of the house. I couldn't afford to move to a new place once Reuben left—I inherited this house from my aunt, and I didn't want to go anywhere anyway. This is *my* house, and I'd loved my aunt. She'd been my surrogate mom and my counselor after my parents moved to Ohio when I started college here. I used the excuse of replacing aging fixtures to erase the memory of Reuben from it.

Ben leans close to watch me. His hands are hard but not rough—he taps computer keyboards all day. But he isn't frail or soft. I've watched him haul around heavy pieces of hardware and tear apart and replace walls to rewire the network.

His warmth distracts me. I miss a spine and have to go back for it.

Our heads almost whack together. We pull back, grinning, but now we're an inch apart, my hands stilling.

Ben draws a finger along my jaw. I surge closer to him.

The touch of his breath, then his lips, makes me drop the tweezers, which rattle in the sink.

I let them stay there while Ben kisses me.

My body had been tired from dancing, but a new energy surges through me, one that has me pulling Ben into my arms. His lips part mine, and the kiss turns deep.

My pounding heart burns. I want to gasp for breath, but I'd have to break this phenomenal kiss to do it.

Ben pulls me closer. The sink digs into my hip, but I don't mind as I'm now standing hard against him. I feel something else hard, sense the need in his touch.

I ease from the kiss. Ben opens his eyes, the intensity in them igniting the yearning I've had for weeks.

I want to move this to the bedroom, but I'm far too timid to ask. Ben doesn't say a word, but when he looks at me, I know he feels the same.

He takes me by the hand and leads me there.

My bedroom is girly, but it's what I wanted after Reuben departed. He'd have hated the gauzy bed hangings and all the pillows, the embroidered flower pieces my aunt had framed for the wall. It had felt good to re-hang the embroidery done by her hands once Reuben was gone.

Ben is out of place in my room, but he doesn't appear to mind. I toss throw pillows to the floor before Ben lays me down on the bed and comes over me. He takes his time, stroking my breast with one gentle hand while he kisses me.

I slide my foot up his leg, indicating I don't necessarily want to go slow. I've been lusting over Ben for a while—if this is going to happen, why wait any longer?

I try to drag him down to me, but Ben disentangles himself. "Hang on a sec."

He lifts away, and I'm cold without him. I remove my glasses and put them on the nightstand, pretending I'm not worried he's about to walk away.

Ben digs his wallet from his back pocket and flushes bright red when he pulls a condom from it.

I laugh. I can't help it. He looks so funny—ashamed and pleased at the same time.

"Austin insists I go packing, no matter what." He tosses the condom to the nightstand and tucks away the wallet. "Even if I'm spending Saturday night alone at the grocery store. *You never know,* Austin says. He's a dickhead."

"I see." I'm giddy. "Do you seduce many women at the grocery store? I hear it's a good place to pick up chicks."

"Chicks?" Ben's smile crinkles his eyes. "Who the hell says that? And no. I don't go out much."

"Me either." I point my toes in my sneakers. "I'm always dancing."

"I bet you don't mean at a club. Also a good place to pick up girls. Or guys. I hear."

I widen my eyes. "People go to clubs and dance? You mean like, with other people?"

"That's what I'm told." Ben shrugs. "I wouldn't know."

"We both like to stay at home then." I hope I'm right. "That's not such a bad thing."

"Lots of good things to do at home." Ben yanks off his shoes. "Work on a program, catch up on reading. This." He waves his hand at me and the bed.

"There's also talking, but I think we should do that later."

"Agreed."

Ben comes back down to me, shoeless, and we share another long, scorching kiss.

This is really happening. I run my hands down his strong back, tugging his shirt out of my way so I can find his skin. He releases my mouth so he can kiss my neck, sending fire through my veins.

I need this man. I haven't *needed* in a long time. I realize I've been working hard at both the office and dance so I can ignore physical desires, or at least I tell myself I can ignore them.

It's been so long since I felt anything at all with a man that I believed myself numb. Now my heart's banging, my body shaking. I'm excited for the first time in forever.

Ben licks my throat. "You're a paradox."

"No one's ever called me that before," I say nervously. "What do you mean? That is, I know what a paradox is ..."

Ben continues through my babbling. "You're slender but so strong." He runs a hand down my abdomen. "And at the same time, light. It's like you flew when I watched you tonight."

"Thank you." The greatest compliment a dancer can receive is that what we do seems effortless. It's not —there's grunting and struggle and pain—but we hide that under makeup and our stage face. But it should *look* effortless.

Ben studies me, no smiling. "I'm not sweet-talking you, I'm serious. You have so much strength."

He makes me want to cry like a big, loopy baby. Strength, my ass. I've been swimming around, trying to make myself believe I'm wonderful without anyone else in my life. My own best friend.

"So do you." I rest my hands on his warm back. "How else could you lug all that computer stuff around?"

Ben's smile returns. "Now I know you're shitting me."

I start to protest but he silences me with a fiery kiss. Fine by me. I wrap myself around him and enjoy the hell out of the moment.

———

Ben

I CAN'T BELIEVE I'M ON ERIN'S BED, IN HER ARMS.

She's hot, and I'm dying for her but trying to be cool. I should take it slow, like Austin says a lady wants.

To hell with that.

She's already stroking under my shirt, so I slide hers up. She helps, quickly wresting the shirt off over her head. I guess she's in as much a hurry as me.

I wasn't wrong about her strength. Her abdomen is smooth, her shoulders tight. I wriggle my hand beneath her black satin bra and unhook it. Erin zips it off before I have the chance to do it for her.

Her breasts are plenty full enough for me—firm and apple-sized, fitting into the hand not stinging from the cactus. Her nipples are dark points, and I lean to take one in my mouth.

I lick her skin, savoring, and suckle her nipple, liking how it tightens in my mouth. At the same time, she's soft all over, skin like satin.

Erin's tugging open my shirt, so I rip the tie from my neck and toss it off. I struggle to disentangle my arms from the sleeves and then send the shirt to the floor after the tie.

We're chest to chest now, bare skin to bare skin. If my heart beats any faster she'll probably call an ambulance.

Next step ... But I can't stop kissing her, so the next step has to wait. I'm dying for her, so I can't wait too long. Damn, that would be embarrassing.

Erin has popped off her shoes while we're kissing, and they hit the ground—*thud, thud*. I reach between us and undo the button of her shorts.

I expect Erin to stop, maybe push me away, say we're going too fast. She holds me closer instead, her fingers pressing my back.

We kiss hungrily, no more teasing. I study Erin's beautiful face, and something inside tells me this is right. The rightest thing I've ever done.

I lift from her and glide her shorts down. While she raises herself on her elbows, watching me, I get out of my pants and underwear as fast as I can. I understand why people do this in the dark—I'm blushing like hell.

She lets her gaze rest on my cock, which is sticking straight out. *It* isn't blushing.

Erin's so beautiful that I stop thinking about myself and my embarrassment. I look at her, and nothing else matters.

She's so still as she surveys me. I think maybe we'll freeze like this, staring at each other, nothing else ever happening—and then she slides off her underwear.

I'm not sure how I get on the bed. To this day, I don't remember. But I'm there with Erin, my knees on either side of her hips. I have the condom ready, sliding it on, Erin helping me.

Now I'm with her, at her opening, she regarding me steadily with her arresting eyes.

When she gives me her little smile, I know I am exactly where I should be.

I softly kiss her while I ease inside.

My world changes. Now I know I've waited all my life to be here, with Erin.

Feeling takes over thoughts. She's tight, sweetly tight, and I can't contain my groans. From the way her face softens, I know she's thinking this is right too. I kiss her, bracing myself on my arms, and start to love her.

Chapter Four

Ben

SHE'S AMAZING, is my last thought before my body takes over.

I'm kissing Erin, pumping into her. Her cries join mine as she meets my thrusts, her breasts soft against my chest.

My knees are burning on the mattress, and our bodies are scalding where they join. I slide on her, and she holds me. We're yelling, then laughing, then shouting again. Words rings through the room—her name, my name, incoherent bellows of joy.

I could stay here the rest of my life. Erin's holding me, her hands tight on my back. She's kissing me, rising to me, nipping my chin.

She's beautiful. Being inside her fires me up hotter than anything has in my life.

I feel my peak coming and try to prevent it, to

suspend this moment. If I come too fast, I'll have to leave her, and I never want to.

Nothing helps. I want her so bad, I can't stop. My body won't let me.

I curse softly, but I'm coming, thrusting so fast I'm pretty sure I'm shoving the bed across the room. Erin moves against me, and her cries are loud, she peaking at the same time.

This is the best night of my life. I'm yelling her name, telling her how beautiful she is, how hot, how tight. I stop short of saying the L- word, but just barely.

Erin's wordless cries wind through mine. Her face is flushed, her hair tumbling down—I want to wrap myself in her.

Erin's gaze holds me, her eyes starry, as the last of my thrusts spiral down. Now we're breathless, arms around each other, lips meeting in frantic need.

I fall to her, and we roll onto our sides, kissing, nipping, licking, kissing some more, into the quiet of the night.

———

Erin

I WAKE FROM A DARK, HARD SLEEP TO FIND A WARM lump beside me in the bed. I cuddle to it, instinctively wanting the comfort.

As awareness trickles into me I realize it's Ben, softly snoring. I remember the crazy sex we had before we both smacked into sleep, and I smile so hard my face hurts.

It's warm in the room, so I sneak out of bed to open the window. Nights are still decently cool in May, and a breeze wafts inside.

Ben's snores cut off, and he wakes.

I quickly slide beneath the sheets, back to his side. "Just letting in some air," I whisper.

He rolls onto his back and scrubs his face. "I should go."

"Why don't you stay?" I say quickly. "I mean, no reason for you to drive around in the wee hours. Stay for breakfast. Or, well, I don't have any food, so we can go out."

He's staring at me while I jabber like I've lost my mind. I'm pretty sure he's going to bail, say *It's been fun*, and take off.

Then he slides the covers back up. "Sure."

"Good." I settle myself on the pillow, drape one arm over his body as I nuzzle in his shoulder. "Too bad we only have one condom."

"Yeah. I'll have to get some more."

I go quiet as my heart squeezes. Does he mean he wants to do this again? Soon?

I hope like hell he does. Ben becomes quiet too, and I wonder if he's spooked himself. I decide that the least said, the better, so I pretend to drift off to sleep.

In a few moments, I feel his lips in my hair. "Good night, Erin."

I don't answer, because I'm supposed to be asleep. But everything inside me is dancing.

———

IN THE MORNING, BEN AND I SHOWER. WE DO IT together, with a lot of kissing and caressing. I learn that day that even if we decide not to have full-blown sex, we can sure do a lot. We touch, kiss, and stroke until we're both high on pleasure, the water scouring us clean.

Tired and damp, we dress and make our way to Ben's truck to head to breakfast.

My across-the-street neighbor, Mrs. Hampton, is out in her front yard, watering her roses. Roses bloom all through spring here, and her bushes are bursting with vibrant red, yellow, and pink.

She stares at me, hose running, as Ben and I emerge from the house.

"Erin?" she calls across our quiet street. "Good morning."

"Hi, Mrs. Hampton." My face is hot, and I feel like a teenager caught making out with a boy. "This is Ben McLaughlin. A ... friend."

"More than a friend, honey." Mrs. Hampton flashes a knowing smile and goes back to watering. "Nice to meet you, Ben. Hope to see more of you."

"Nice to meet you too, Mrs. Hampton," Ben says without a qualm. "We're off to get some breakfast. Want us to bring you anything?"

Mrs. Hampton looks up in surprise, then nods a little more cordially. "Thank you. No, I don't need anything. You have fun."

Ben opens the door for me to get into his truck, then climbs in the driver's side. He waves to Mrs. Hampton, who stares as she raises her hand in return, the water from her hose splashing on the front walk instead of the roses.

"Thanks for being nice to her," I say to Ben as we pull out. "She was a good friend of my aunt, and she's kind of protective of me."

Ben shrugs. "I'm nice to everybody. Plus, I like being the bad-ass who spent the night with a hot lady."

I shake my head. "You are so full of shit."

"No, I'm not. You're one seriously hot chick."

I laugh as I recall our banter from the night before. "You need to get out of your computer closet more."

"Why? I like it in there." Ben heads west on Glendale toward a breakfast place I've told him about. "My brothers never darken the door—too scared. But you can come in any time."

I don't answer, but keep smiling.

Inside, I'm a little uneasy. What happens when we go back to work Monday? Do we keep this a secret? Or will Ben reveal our liaison and open us to teasing from his entire family?

Or will he even want to talk about it? Is this a one-night-stand, or what? I'm not sure, because I've never had a one-night-stand before.

I decide to live in the moment. We head to my

breakfast place on Seventh Street, where I go often enough to be greeted by name. The staff gawps at Ben, and I watch them decide that the shy girl finally came out of her shell.

We're served their signature pancakes, and the waitress brings me an extra muffin, on the house. She winks as she walks away.

I break the muffin—blueberry, my favorite—in half, and share it with Ben. It feels nice, dividing things between us. I always dine here alone.

"How's your hand?" I ask him.

Ben glances at it and wriggles his fingers, as though he's forgotten his injury. "Fine. It's fine."

"Good."

Wonderful. We've had wild, amazing sex, and suddenly we can't exchange more than inanities.

"I have a matinee at two," I remark as we chow down on the pancakes and muffin.

Ben checks his watch—a real one on his wrist, with a dial and hands, old-school. "It's only ten. You won't be late."

"Oh, I'm not worried. Just letting you know." *So it won't be tense when we say good-bye. So you know I'm not leaving because I'm tired of this ... whatever it is.*

"Want me to drive you?" Ben asks.

My face heats. "You don't have to. I do own a car."

"I don't mind. I could stay for the show."

Now I'm seriously squirming. "I wouldn't make you sit through that again, if you didn't want to."

Ben looks mildly surprised then returns to his muffin. "It's a great show. You're an amazing dancer."

I will melt through the floor if he keeps this up. "It's mostly kids and seniors who go to the matinees."

"Meaning I'll stand out." Ben shrugs. "I like kids and seniors." He glances up and meets my gaze, dismay entering his expression. "Unless you don't want me to come."

"I didn't say that." I'd love him there. Knowing he was in the audience last night had made me feel both nervous and supported at the same time, as though his presence held me up. "I won't stop you—I just wasn't sure you'd enjoy it."

"You let me worry about that."

"Well, okay."

We study each other a few more minutes, then we both flush and continue our breakfast.

"I was thinking we might stop by a drugstore," Ben says after a time.

I start coughing. I grab a napkin and plaster it to my face so I won't spew crumbs all over the place. Once my fit is over, I lower the napkin to find Ben regarding me with amusement.

"Why?" I ask him. "Need painkiller for your hand?"

"I think you know why."

Ben's faint smile does me in. He wants to watch me dance, and he wants to prepare for what might happen afterward.

This is all kinds of nerve-wracking, but I've never been happier in my life.

———

Ben

ERIN PRETENDS TO SHOP FOR OTHER THINGS WHEN we visit the nearest drugstore, and we meet up again at my truck after. She doesn't ask me what I bought, and I keep the box of condoms out of sight.

I don't know how my brothers do it. When I hand the box to the cashier—a plump, friendly woman in her fifties—I can't make eye contact with her. I know she's laughing her ass off at me as I run my card through the machine, snatch up the bag, and flee.

Erin doesn't say one word about my purchase. We go to her house where she has enough time to pack up all the stuff she needs. We make a quick stop at my place so I can put on fresh clothes, before we drive to the theater. Erin comes inside and admires my house, which was nothing but a square-box, generic development home before my brothers and I fixed it up. I like having her here—she makes it brighter somehow.

I'd like to linger, but we need to hurry so she won't be late.

Once we arrive at the theater, Erin disappears to get into costume. To kill time before the show starts, I wander around the old-town square. It's hot so not many people are about today, but some go into and out of the library, and others stroll around the green.

I head back to the theater when ticket-holders start to go in. I insisted to Erin that I buy a ticket today because she treated me last night, and I didn't take no for an answer.

The show begins. I'm squeezed in next to a family with three little girls who watch the dancers in awe. On my other side is an older couple who murmur to each other through the start of the show, more interested in each other's opinions than what's happening onstage. They're also holding hands.

When Erin comes on, I surge forward in my seat.

She's as stunning as ever, her elegance enchanting, but I noticed she's a little distracted. I remember enough from last night's performance to see that she misses a few steps in her solo dance, and again when she's with Dean.

Shit, is this because of me? Erin had tried to persuade me not to come today—maybe she really doesn't want me there.

I hear too much sex can throw an athlete off their game. Not that I'd know—I was in the computer club while the jocks were out playing football with my brothers.

My heart squeezes. Am I going to have to walk away from Erin, pretend our incredible night never happened, to save her career?

No, no, no. What am I thinking? Shit like that only happens in movies.

Then again, what do I know? I've had girlfriends before, but I've never spontaneously jumped into bed with a woman. Not that it was entirely spontaneous—I've been drooling after Erin since she started working in our office a month ago.

But if I'm distracting her so much she can't dance, what chance do we have together? I know that if Erin has to choose between dancing and me, I'll be out in the cold so fast I won't have time to shiver.

I try to tell myself that Erin missing steps has nothing to do with me, but I'm scared that it does. I white-knuckle the rest of the performance. When it's over—after the bowing, the flower giving, and the director greeting the kids from a local dance school—I head to the stage.

The security guy from last night is there again. This time, he gives me a cordial nod and sends me right up the stairs to the wings.

Dean spots me and hurries over. Not like he wants to greet me, but as though he's trying to head me off. What the hell?

A glance past Dean's large frame tells me why he's so worried. Just outside the hall that leads to the dressing rooms is Erin. With her is another man—a black-haired, handsome guy with enough hard muscles to tell me he's a dancer.

He has Erin in his arms, and as I watch, he leans down and gives her a passionate kiss on the mouth.

Chapter Five

Erin

"WHAT THE HELL are you doing here?" I all but yell once I finally pry Reuben off me.

Reuben Barrow gives me his best slick smile as I wipe my mouth in disgust. I truly never wanted his saliva on me again.

"Aren't you happy to see me?" he has the gall to ask. "I'm back, sweetheart. I've signed with Clarice again. You need a decent male dancer in this company."

I brim with fury. Reuben is supposed to be in Milwaukee, with a dance company that begged him to join them two years ago. I wonder how many people he pissed off before they fired him. I'm certain he was fired —he'd been hot to erase the dust of Arizona from his feet, loudly saying he'd never return. He wouldn't be here if he wasn't now desperate for a job.

"Clarice re-hired you?"

"Don't sound so surprised. You know Clarice never wanted me to go. Neither did you, I recall. And here I am."

Reuben spreads his arms, his smile as cool as ever. I guess he expects me to fling myself at him, rejoicing that he's come home.

He'd dumped me plenty fast when the Milwaukee opportunity came along, claiming that long-distance relationships didn't work. I'd protested at first, but when I realized he truly didn't give a shit about me, the scales, as they say, fell from my eyes. I quit fighting the breakup, threw his things in a box, and set the box in the middle of my driveway. The box had vanished overnight, and so had Reuben.

Today, I'd danced on to the stage to do my solo and spied Reuben in the wings on the other side, next to Clarice. What a way to throw me off my game. My performance sucked, seriously sucked, and I knew it.

And now, worst of all, Dean is bearing down on us with Ben. *Shit.*

"Reuben," Dean booms. "You get tired of all that winter up north? I remember you proclaiming you were done with heat. Welcome back to the sun."

I need to extract myself from the situation. I'll grab Ben, who has halted at Dean's side, taking in Reuben with his assessing gaze, and run, run, run. Maybe never come back.

Damn Reuben. I'm happy in Clarice's dance company, but I never want to work with him again. Or even lay eyes him.

"Wisconsin wasn't so bad." Reuben shrugs. "I was working all the time, so I didn't notice the weather. It's already too damned hot here, and it's only May."

"So stay inside and work," Dean says. "How about we have a beer and catch up?"

Dean is wonderful. He's trying to steer Reuben away from me, but Reuben digs in his heels. "I was thinking about catching up with Erin."

"Erin's busy," Dean tells him.

"Doing what?"

Ben, who is no fool, has figured out what's going on. I haven't told him about Reuben, but anyone can see he's an ex. I hope I'm conveying clearly that I want nothing to do with the idiot.

Dean's trying, but Reuben won't go away.

"This is Ben," I say loudly. "Ben McLaughlin. He's with me."

Ben moves close to my side, facing Reuben.

Ben has height—all the McLaughlin brothers do. Ben is the shortest, but that means he's about six foot two, compared to his six four brothers. Reuben, like many male dancers, is strong but compact. Dean's on the tall side for a dancer, but Reuben's about average.

Ben towers over him. He gazes down at Reuben, and Reuben takes subtle steps backward so he doesn't have to crick his neck to meet Ben's eyes.

Ben's red-highlighted brown hair is adorably messy, his clothes casual—pants and a polo shirt. Reuben is sleek in a dress shirt and tie, his dark hair combed and gelled. I used to think Reuben was to-die-for handsome, but Ben puts him to shame.

Reuben raises his brows. "What do you mean, *with* you?" He doesn't even say *hello* or *how are you?* like a polite person.

"She means *with* him," Dean supplies. "They have a thing going on."

"Yes," I say hastily. "A thing." I hope Ben doesn't turn around and stride off in disgust.

Ben slides his arm around me. My heart leaps with relief and joy.

He says nothing, but Ben doesn't have to. There's advantage to being the silent type. At least with Reuben, who can't handle having to guess what people think.

"A serious thing," Deans continues. "We're blown away by it. Can't wait to see what happens next."

He's laying it on a little thick, but Ben, bless him, remains rock solid. "Nice to meet you," he tells Reuben.

"Sure." Reuben looks confused. He glances at Dean. "Same old gossip, aren't you, Dean? Why don't you go put on your fairy godmother costume?"

Dean had worn that at a party once, as a joke. Dean beams him a big smile. "You know, you have a pretty face, Barrow. I'd hate to ruin it with my giant fist."

"I think it's time to go," Ben says. He keeps his arm around me and steers me past Dean, Reuben, and the dancers who have paused to watch the drama. "See you, Dean." He jerks his chin. "Reuben."

Dean bars Reuben's way as I walk off with Ben, though I'm not sure Reuben would have tried to follow. He does have some pride—barrels of it, actually.

"I have to change," I whisper to Ben.

"No problem. Want me to guard the door?" He gives me a half smile, but I see the anger in his eyes.

"There's a sofa outside. Or you can take off—I can get a ride home with Ida."

"Not with Mr. Wonderful hanging around. I'll take you home. What is he? Your ex?"

My face is hot. "Bad break-up. I'll ..." We've reached the dressing room door. "This is me."

"I'll be waiting."

I open my mouth to tell him he doesn't have to, that I'll understand if he high-tails it outta here.

Ben pulls me close, hand on the back of my neck, and kisses me on the mouth. It's a rocking kiss, and my troubles dissipate as I ride on it. Ben knows how to kiss —he takes his time, infusing me with warmth.

I'm breathless when Ben pulls away and gives me his crooked smile.

"I'll be waiting," he repeats.

I manage a nod then edge backwards into the dressing room. It's hard to close the door and leave him out, but I share this small dressing room with three other dancers, and I can't let him in. The door shuts, the click of the latched drowned in the voices of the dancers chattering excitedly about today's performance and the gathering afterward.

Ben

"SO ... BEN, IS IT? WHAT DO YOU DO?"

I figured the asshole would find me sooner or later, not difficult in the small maze of backstage halls. I lounge on the arm of the sofa Erin pointed out to me, checking my messages.

One from my mom asking me to pick up something for the office, one from Zach saying he hasn't heard from me all weekend, and what's up?

I'm answering Zach evasively when I hear Reuben's voice, see his feet halt a yard from the sofa.

I take my time pressing *Send* on Zach's message before I raise my head. "Computer engineer."

"Yeah?" Reuben blinks, obviously not expecting that answer. "I didn't think computer guys were into dance."

I shrug. "I'm into a lot of things."

"Including Erin?"

The smirk on the smug bastard's face annoys me. It's a good thing I grew up with Austin, who has an ego that can bust open doors. Austin, however, is a good guy deep down. Will do anything for anyone. And he isn't smarmy.

Keeping up with Austin's certainty that he's God's gift to women lets me survey Reuben with some detachment. He is, I guess, good-looking in a way women like, with his dark hair and symmetrical face, plus he has a dancer's body and easy way of carrying himself.

Too bad he's a dickhead.

"Not really your business," I say mildly.

"No?" Reuben steps nearer. "We broke up only because I had to move up north, and we knew a long-distance relationship wouldn't work." He's even closer now, in my personal space. If he touches me, I'm decking him. "But now I'm home."

"I see that." I'm not good with snappy comebacks so I keep my answers short and simple.

"Erin needs someone who understands her." Reuben takes a step back, lucky him. "Not a geek focused on his device." He gives a flick of a hand at my phone, twisting his lip at his double-entendre.

"Got it."

"Good." Reuben gives me a once over. I remain on the sofa's arm—I'm almost eye-to-eye with him at this height. His regards me in disdain, and I make myself not care. "I'm glad you understand," he says.

"Oh, I understand." I slide my phone into my back pocket and stand up. I like the hint of worry in his eyes as I stare down at him. "I understand that Erin lives her own life and makes her own decisions about who she's with. What *you* should understand is that, if you mess with Erin, you mess with me."

"Are you threatening me?" Reuben widens his dark eyes and draws himself up. "Do you know who you're talking to?"

Growing up with three sports-involved brothers—I

was Zach's practice tackle dummy when he was into football—means I don't even skip a heartbeat. I can tell Reuben's strong, as dancers are, but I learned to fight back early in my life.

"Yeah ... Reuben, is it?"

He drops the *I'm-so-sophisticated* pose and leans to me again, becoming nothing more than a pissed-off brat who sees a threat to his position in life.

"You watch yourself," he snarls at me. "I don't give many people second chances."

Is he going to throw a punch at me right here in the hall, with dancers and theater staff wandering around us?

Whatever would have happened, I don't know, because Dean barrels out of a dressing room a few doors down. With the makeup wiped from his face, Dean looks human. Not as handsome as Reuben—his face is hard and bears lines of experience—but he's bigger than Reuben, with more magnetism.

"Come on, Reuben," Dean says jovially but with force. "Let me buy you that drink before you get your ass kicked."

Reuben straightens up, annoyed at the interruption. "I don't date guys, Dean. I've told you before. Many times."

"Like I'd go out with you." Dean huffs a laugh. "I have taste. What I mean is the company is heading for happy hour. I'm inviting you along, giving you a chance for a graceful exit. Erin's done with you. Get over it."

Reuben glowers at him. "Fuck you, Dean."

He turns on his heel and stalks down the hall, banging open a door at the far end. Bright sunlight flashes into the windowless corridor, then cuts off as the door slams.

Dean gives the closed door the finger and turns back to me. "Sorry about that, Ben. You're invited to happy hour too, now that I got rid of Reuben."

"Thanks." I glance at the dressing room door through which Erin disappeared. "Not sure what Erin wants to do."

"I get it." Dean flashes a big smile and thumps me on the shoulder. "See you there. Or not."

He walks away, chuckling. I rub my shoulder, thinking that if Dean ever decided to kick my ass, I'd be hard-pressed to survive.

———

"I don't want to talk about it," Erin tells me as she settles into my truck, buckling her seatbelt.

"Okay," I answer.

In silence, I pull out of the lot and navigate the traffic that has built up even on a Sunday afternoon. There's a train chugging across the five-way intersection behind us, which is stopping cars in all directions.

Erin deflates. "I'm sorry. I didn't mean to sound harsh. It's just that—we broke up, Reuben left, and I realized it was a good thing. I'm done with it."

"Okay."

Erin gazes at me in concern. I turn off Fifty-Ninth

Avenue to get away from traffic and wind through a quiet neighborhood to emerge onto Fifty-First, a calmer way to go.

"Okay as in we're good?" Erin asks anxiously. "Or okay as in you never want to speak to me again?"

I send her a look of amazement. "As in we're good. Why wouldn't I want to speak to you again?" *Or kiss you, or have fantastic sex with you?*

My body is still on fire from being with her, and I think I'll never calm it down.

"I don't want you to think less of me because I fell for Reuben," Erin says.

I recall how the guy acted like Erin was his property, and my anger rises—at him, not her. "It happens," I manage to say.

"I can't believe now that I ever admired him. But before, Reuben was nice, actually. Supportive. In fact, he helped me get my job in Clarice's company. But when he saw the opportunity to make it big on his own, he couldn't leave fast enough."

I slant Erin a sideways glance. "I thought you didn't want to talk about it."

Her face grows pink. "I don't, but I want you to understand. I was excited to be dancing, to have the opportunity to be with West Valley, and I guess I was grateful to him. Kind of blinded me to Reuben's faults. Most professional dance troupes take dancers right out of high school. I was already considered too old by many when I started searching for a dance job after college. Clarice is different—she wants skilled performers, not people she has to mold. And she hired me, thanks to Reuben."

"I get that."

Erin skewers me with a skeptical look. "No, you don't. You're wondering why the hell I ever trusted a man like him."

"Maybe. But I know that guys don't always understand what women see in other guys."

Erin tucks a loose lock of hair behind her ear. "I suppose that's true. Women don't understand why men fall for skanky bitches either."

I have to grin. "Skanky bitches? I don't think I've ever met one. But then, they avoid nerds."

"Can't think why. Unless they're stupid."

I tap the steering wheel. "I think you just gave me a compliment. Not sure. Did you?"

Erin's smile blossoms, which makes everything better. "Yes."

"That's why I'm in my truck with you, not a skanky bitch." I make her laugh, which releases something inside me. "Interested in Dean's happy hour?"

Erin shakes her head. "Not really. He's a hard charger—dancing and partying are Dean's life. I just want to take a nap."

"That can be arranged. Want me to drop you at home?"

Erin goes very quiet. When traffic lets me, I turn my head to see her watching me, her mouth straight, her eyes soft.

"Only if you come in," she answers. "You did stop at the drugstore."

Immediately, my body is ready, willing, and able. If it weren't for Phoenix traffic barreling around me, I'd pull off somewhere and do it right now. A lot of places are closed on Sunday—I bet I can find a quiet parking lot.

I keep myself contained until we pull into the driveway of Erin's house. Mrs. Hampton across the street is nowhere in sight, and I breathe a sigh of relief. Not that she isn't watching out her window.

I park the truck and we hop out, my legs shaking with the effort of holding myself back.

Erin unlocks the front door and ushers me gently inside.

Chapter Six

Erin

THE REST of the afternoon is bliss. Ben and I lay in the
sunshine in my bed, getting up only to eat—ordering
out pizza—and then hitting the mattress again. I forget
all about Reuben, my tired body, my worries.

All I need is right here in this room.

Ben eventually rises to leave, late in the night. It's
quiet outside as we emerge, moonlight bathing the
street. My neighbors are indoors, and only occasional
distant traffic breaks the silence.

"Good night," Ben whispers.

I rise on tiptoe, put my arms around him, and kiss
him. I want to kiss him for the rest of the night, and
wake up in the morning against him. *Why don't you
stay?* I want to ask. *Forever ...*

But life marches on. We have work in the morning
—Ben needs to go home and get ready for that. No one

knows about us and our secret weekend. As Ben eases from the kiss and rests his forehead against mine, I wonder if he'll want to keep it secret.

We study each other, Ben holding my hands. I don't want to let go. Finally, he releases me, reluctantly I think, and turns away.

I stand in the driveway and watch him back out and roll away. I wave until his truck is out of sight, though it's too dark for him to see me.

The house feels empty when I go back inside, but different as well. Serene. A new warmth has entered it. I straighten up the kitchen and go to bed, but I don't sleep. I think of Ben, lying in his own house a couple miles away, turn my face to the pillow where he slept, and sigh in contentment.

———

I WALK INTO WORK MONDAY MORNING A LITTLE flustered. I arrive early as I always do to unlock the doors and turn on the lights. I make coffee in the break room then check the company's phone and email messages. I'll deliver each message to the appropriate McLaughlin when they arrive, except for the generic questions I can now answer myself.

I like my job. It's not glamorous, and it won't make me rich and famous, but there's something satisfying about helping out at McLaughlin Renovations. The family is easy to work with, and they're nice to me. The brothers have their own light squabbles, but they manage to keep things professional at work, and they appreciate what I do.

I don't want to ruin a good thing. Plus, I need the paycheck, because while dance is wonderful and fulfilling, Clarice can't pay us lavishly, and the cost of living is fairly high. Everyone in the company has a day job.

I struggle to keep my concentration on my computer and the phone and not worry about how I'll act when Ben gets here.

Austin breezes in, greeting me cheerfully on his way to coffee. Ryan arrives, looking relaxed—no doubt due to what the newlyweds did all weekend. I smile to myself as I return his "Good morning."

Zach and Abby rush in slightly late, flushed and breathless. I give Abby a wink as she sails by, and she laughs. Zach clears his throat and dives into his office.

I don't see Ben. Maybe he decided not to come in today. My heart beats faster. If not, why not?

But perhaps it's better we don't see each other right away. We can take a step back, figure out how we feel about this past weekend. Maybe it was just a weekend, and we'll move on.

My mouth goes dry. I don't want to move on. I want to see Ben. Talk to him. Even if we only say hello.

"Hey."

I shriek and jump a foot out of my chair. When I land again, Ben is beside me, on my side of the reception desk.

He gives me a baffled look from under hair that needs trimming. "What's wrong?"

"I didn't see you come in. I thought you were staying home today."

"I used the back door. I was carrying in some new equipment."

"Oh."

My wild speculations and fears suddenly seem stupid. Ben pulls up the extra chair behind my desk, just as he does whenever he's come to give me a computer lesson.

I scoot closer to him, inhaling his clean scent—soap and toothpaste, no aftershave or cologne. I start to say hello more politely when his mom wafts in and pauses by the desk.

"There you are, Ben," Virginia says. She's a trim woman in her late fifties, her face retaining the beauty I've seen in her wedding photos from nearly forty years ago. Her hair is dark like Austin's, her eyes the blue of all her sons. "I was just about to ask if you'll start training Erin on the orders software. She's ready for that, I think."

I warm with her praise—I like that Virginia trusts me more and more with the business. I hope she can hire me on permanently, and that me boinking one of her sons won't change her mind.

Ben and I keep our faces straight until Virginia scoops up her messages, sails into her office, and closes the door. Then we both burst into quiet laughter.

"Software training," I choke out. "Is that what the kids are calling it these days?"

"Seems as good a term as any."

We go quiet. Ben isn't in a hurry to grab my mouse and start darting the cursor around the screen. My setup is pretty basic—in Ben's office he has multiple screens, racks of computers, the latest tablets, and gadgets I don't even recognize. At my desk it's monitor, keyboard, and mouse.

My chair squeaks, and I quickly still myself.

"So," I ask softly. "Is it awkward?"

Ben's voice is as hushed as mine. "Why does it have to be awkward?"

Because we've slept together. The quiet receptionist had glorious sex with the introverted IT guy, and we both work for IT guy's parents.

"I don't know," I admit.

"What's up, peeps?" Austin strides out, coffee in hand, to attack the mail stacked on the counter. "Wild weekend, Erin? Missed you at the family Sunday dinner yesterday. Hoped you'd be there so I'd have someone to talk to besides the besotted couples. Ben ditched too …"

Austin peers over the high counter at us, sitting close together, looking up at him in trepidation. He stares at us a moment, his mouth falling open as he puts the pieces together. He takes a breath … and lets it out again.

"*Okaayy.*" Austin, who prides himself on being the best-looking McLaughlin with his dark hair and blue eyes, taps his wad of mail on the counter. "So, I'll just be walking away now."

He moves from the desk in slow, deliberate steps,

exaggerating a casual walk. When he reaches the middle of the showroom, be begins to whistle, which he keeps up all the way to his office. The door clicks shut.

Ben huffs a laugh. "All right, so it's awkward."

"What do we do?" I whisper.

He leans closer. "We play it cool."

I don't know how I can play it cool when his breath ruffles my hair and he kisses me below the ear. I want to turn to him, grab him, rip off his clothes, and make wild, passionate love to him under the desk.

Imagining it makes me laugh. Ben laughs with me, and soon have our arms over our stomachs, half falling out of our chairs. I wave my hand in front of my face.

"Stop, stop, stop. Show me ordering. You're supposed to be ..."

We laugh again, and can't cease. Abby is heading out, and pauses at the desk. The diamond on her third finger sparkles.

"You two sound happy," Abby says, interested. "What's the joke?"

I shake my head, and Ben wipes his eyes. "No joke," he says. "Just ... um ... a software thing."

Abby starts to shrug, then she, like Austin, hesitates. I know I'm turning all shades of red, and then I fear there's a hickey on my neck from where Ben suckled it last night. I think I'd have noticed it when dressing this morning though. Wouldn't I?

I self-consciously put my hand on my throat, pretending I'm cupping my chin. Ben doesn't help, because he's red too, staring hard at the computer screen, which is blank, the McLaughlin logo floating around the black background.

Abby straightens. "Well," she says with exaggerated brightness. "I'm off to a radio station downtown. Ad meeting. Be back after lunch."

"Okay." I quickly make a note. "Good luck."

"Mmm-hmm." Abby looks us over one more time, then strolls out, high heels clicking.

Ben and I gaze at each other. "Don't you dare start laughing." I point at him. "We'll never get anything done today."

"Somehow, I don't really care." Ben leans back, hands behind his head.

"Should we tell them?" I approach the question with caution.

"Tell who what?"

I fold my fingers into my palms. "Your family. That we're ..."

Having fantastic sex? Dating? That's a tame word for this weekend. And was it a one-time thing? I have no idea. Ben isn't the type who lays out exactly what he's thinking. Reuben had simply moved in with me and hadn't budged from my house until he found another job. I realized after he left he'd been simply mooching off me.

Ben is far more independent, with a nice place of his own. A family he's close to. I'm the interloper. Abby and Calandra have been friends of the family a long time, with past histories with Zach and Ryan.

"No." Ben's abrupt word cuts into my thoughts.

"No, what?"

"I don't want to tell them." Ben brings his hands down, the chair rocking forward as he leans close. "I want this between us, for now. My family can be seriously nosy."

That was an understatement. Nothing happened but all the brothers, and Alan and Virginia, soon knew about it. Great Aunt Mary knew whatever everyone else didn't. It was uncanny how gossip whipped around the family.

"Want to have lunch?" Ben's next question drags my attention to him.

I glance quickly at the clock on my desk. "It's nine-thirty."

A chuckle. "I mean at lunch. Want to go grab something?"

"Yes." The word leaves my mouth with enthusiasm. Then, dismay. "No, I can't."

Ben blinks. "I like that you can surprise me."

"I already promised a friend I'd meet her for lunch. You met her, in the scrum. Ida—she's a dancer. She's the head elf. In the show, I mean."

"There are elves?" Ben looks confused.

"Clarice's shows are kind of abstract. But yes, she was in the red and gold. Anyway, we made this date a while ago, and I can't cancel on her."

"No." Ben lifts his hands. "Don't want you to do that. Go. Have fun."

"Tomorrow," I say quickly. "We can have lunch together tomorrow."

Ben nods, his grin returning. "It's a date."

We watch each other, the laughter threatening to return. It's so easy, laughing with Ben. As though everything we think and say is funny.

It isn't funny—the laughter is from giddiness. Something I haven't felt in a long time.

I'd forgotten how nice it is to fall in love.

"Orders," I say with determination. "Your mom is going to expect me to understand how to do the orders."

Ben lets out a breath. "Okay. Here we go." He clicks the mouse with hands that touched me so well Saturday night and throughout Sunday.

Working here will never be the same again.

————

Ben

When Erin takes off for lunch, I head back to my cave and try to concentrate on installing a couple new pieces of hardware. Usually I get absorbed in that, but today all I can think of are Erin's eyes behind her glasses when she smiled at me before she left and said, "See you later."

I'd wanted to kiss her. We'd been standing in the middle of the office with my family streaming to and fro, Ryan talking with a client.

I wished I could say to hell with everything and kiss her. Take her in my arms, run my hands down her back to cup her fine ass and kiss her deeply.

But I didn't want to embarrass her, so I just nodded and let her go.

My brothers and parents have already drifted off to lunch, Ryan and Dad with the client, Zach joining Abby after her meeting. The only one left is Austin, who's in his office singing along enthusiastically with whoever he's playing on his radio. I stopped listening to popular music a long time ago, preferring blues classics. True music.

I lay down my screwdriver, dust off my pants, take a swift swig from a bottle of water, and head to his office.

When I walk in, Austin breaks off his wailing and turns down the volume. "Oh, sorry. Didn't know anyone was still here."

I lean against the doorframe. "Felt like staying in. Hey, can I talk to you?"

"Sure. What about?"

Austin is the brother I'm least connected with. Zach and I are closest, we two middle brothers finding common ground. Like I said, I was Zach's tackle dummy all through high school, but he taught me a lot about football and holding my own. I couldn't catch a ball to save my life, but I was good at running and punching, which made the other kids learn respect.

Austin, though. He's about dressing in sharp suits and going to clubs and having the most beautiful women in town on his arm. He's a schmoozer, but a decent guy if you catch him on a good day.

"How do you do it?" I ask.

"How do I do what?"

"You know." I wave my hand vaguely. "Be you. With women."

Austin is baffled. "I don't know. Talk to them?"

"Yeah, but specifically? How do you know exactly what to say to them, how to treat them, what to do?"

Austin stares blankly as though I've asked him to explain particle physics. Then he has an "aha" moment.

"This is about Erin, isn't it?" Austin launches himself from his chair and comes around the desk. "I knew there was something up with you two. What happened—did you hook up?"

I don't like that term—*hook-up*. So impersonal, like the encounter is all about sex and nothing else. I try to keep my expression neutral, disapproving even, but my face feels hot.

Austin is overjoyed. "You *did* hook up. That's awesome, bro." He grabs me in a bear hug, pounding me on the back. "You dog." He stands back, admiring. "She won't even look at me."

"Leave her alone." I'm all defensive, my fists balling. "Do not say a word to her, all right?"

Austin lifts his hands. "Sure, sure. No problem. The secret is safe with me. But why are you asking my advice if you've already scored?"

Scored. Another term I don't like. "I don't know where to go from here. What do I do? Buy her flowers? Take her to a fancy dinner? I want her to like me."

"From what I saw this morning she seems to like you well enough. But I get you. You don't want her to stop." He sobers. "I have to tell you though, you don't want to lavish too much attention on her. Don't come off as needy. You want her chasing *you*."

I eye him doubtfully. "This works for you, does it?"

"Well enough. But why are you so worried? You've had girlfriends before."

"Not like this." No woman in my life—the few that have been in my life—can compare.

"True. Erin's a class act. Not that your other girl-friends weren't," Austin adds hastily. "There was Debra in high school ..."

"Now married to a rich property developer."

"And Jean in college—your lab partner, right?"

"Traveling the world as a photojournalist. Gave up computers for the road."

"Hmm." Austin leans back against his desk, hands supporting him. "I can see your problem. Great women, but they pick someone or something else over you."

"Yeah, that's how I roll."

"Don't be gloomy. I saw how Erin smiled at you. All right—what does she like to do?"

"Dance." I warm inside. "I went to her show this weekend. Twice. She's amazing."

I must look seriously impressed, because Austin grins at me. "What else?"

"As far as I know, she dances and she works here. If Erin ever has to choose between dance and our busi-ness, she'll blow us off so fast we won't know what happened."

Austin watches me closely. "Something else is bugging you, because you know you can still be with her even if she chooses not to work for us. What?"

I don't want to dump my doubts on him, but heave a sigh. "All right, there's this guy. Her ex. Good-looking, apparently a great dancer, used to live with her. Erin says she's done with him, and he is kind of a dick, but —" I spread my arms. "Then there's me. The gawky guy who forgets to comb his hair. I spend all day in my den. What the hell do I have to offer a woman like Erin?" I drop my hands to my sides. "You gotta help me, bro."

Chapter Seven

Erin

"SO, TELL ME ALL ABOUT BEN." Ida, my partner in crime in Clarice's dance company eyes me over her latte.

"What about him?" I'm suddenly reluctant. "You met him."

We've been talking about everything *but* Ben—how the performances went this weekend, what Ida heard about Clarice's idea for a new show in the fall, and Reuben's sudden and annoying return. Nothing about Ben.

"I met him really briefly." Ida leans forward, risking smearing whipped cream on a deep blue shirt that matches her eyes. "Then he drove you home, leaving me high and dry." Ida laughs, clearly not put out. "And then ..." She waggles her brows.

"Then what? Why are you so nosy all of the sudden?"

"Why are you so bashful all of the sudden? I'm interested. Mostly because a) he's cute, and b) I haven't seen you this happy in a while. I like this new, bubbly Erin."

"Bubbly?" My face is scalding enough to heat the coffee. "I hope I'm not bubbly."

"Effervescent, then. You danced so well on Saturday night, it was like you were born for the part. Dean couldn't shut up about how well you did. So when we went to Freida's after the party, we threw him into her pool."

I burst out laughing. I hadn't known that. "He never said a word."

"He loved it. Dean swims like a fish. He pretended to need help out, then started pulling other people in with him. Anyway, I wondered where you'd suddenly obtained this sparkle. When I saw you with Ben again yesterday—I knew."

"We're not a couple," I say quickly.

"Sure. Because why else would he run interference with Reuben and wait to escort you out, like a gentleman? If you're not a couple, you're close to it."

Ida has been there for me through it all—my first terrified rehearsals and shows with the company, my infatuation with and then disappointment in Reuben, the breakup, the house makeover, the bad jobs I've had with the temp agency, the great job I was sent to with the McLaughlins, and worry about taking over the lead part this weekend. I owe her the truth, but I'm reluctant, mostly because I don't know what the truth is.

"All right, all right." I let my voice go low, so the guys in ties having lunch at the next table don't hear all about my love life. "We did have Saturday night together. And Sunday morning. And Sunday afternoon ..."

Ida's mouth is open, her eyes wide with delight. "Seriously? Wow, the best friend is the last to know. I figured you were into Ben, and he's into you, but I had no idea it was ..." She leans closer to hiss, "Consummated."

She does get cream on her shirt that time. Ida absently picks up a napkin and wipes it away.

"Yes, but ..." I delicately sip the unsweetened iced tea I ordered with my salad. "It was wonderful, don't get me wrong. But I don't know if it's going any further."

"Why not?" Ida's eyes narrow. "Wait, you mean, because of Reuben? Please, please, please tell me you aren't thinking of getting back with that turd."

She says it loudly. The guys at the next table glance over with interest.

"Of course not." I keep my voice steady, because I want the listening guys to know my answer. "I don't know what I saw in him in the first place."

"A charming, hot guy who was all over you," Ida says with confidence. "Reuben can lay it on thick. I was half in love with him myself. Then I got to know him. I can tell Ben is so much better, and I only said howdy to him while you two were noshing burgers."

Ben *is* so much better. I realized that when I first laid eyes on him. He's also great in bed, funny, kind, and chivalrous, something not talked about a lot these days.

"I like him." I try to shrug as though it's no big deal. "But it was a weekend. Who knows if it will be anything more?"

My heart burns as I say the words. It's far too late for me to be casual now. If Ben walks away from this, I will hurt far, far worse than I did when Reuben left. Realms beyond that.

Ida knows. I see it in her eyes. She has a long, thin face, which she softens by letting her dark hair hang past it in soft waves. She thoughtfully sips her latte and swipes cream from her lip with her tongue.

"Tell you what you do," she says. "First, get back with Reuben."

I choke, nearly spewing my tea. "What? Why the hell would I do that?" I don't even want to speak to him again. "Who are you and what have you done with my friend?"

"Hear me out. You get back with Reuben, cheat on him with Ben, then kick Reuben to the curb. What's good for the gander ..."

Ida's voice carries, and the guys at the next table are grinning now, not bothering to mind their own business.

"No." I look over at them. "No," I repeat. "Not gonna happen."

"She's too nice," Ida tells the guys. "But Reuben's such an asshole."

The work buddies are laughing at us. They get up, tell us to take it easy, and walk out, heading back to the office.

Like I should be doing.

"I have to work with Ben," I say. "It's very distracting. Office romances never succeed, right?"

"Then quit your job," Ida suggests.

"Sure, cause I don't need that income." I roll my eyes.

"Then jump his bones."

Ida has a solution to everything, but it's not her love life we're talking about.

We finish up and leave the restaurant. Outside, Ida gives me a crushing hug.

"Don't worry about it," she says. "I'm teasing the hell out of you, because it's so nice to see you happy. If you need any help, you let me know."

"Just keep me from going insane."

"Stay away from Reuben, and you'll be fine."

I let out a sigh. "I hope I won't have to dance with him. I'd have to leave the troupe."

Ida squeezes my arms. "Clarice will never pair you with him. She won't put together dancers who hate each other—she doesn't need the drama. Besides, you and Dean are perfect together for now. Fluid." She releases me and moves her arms in a graceful wave. "I'm so jealous."

"I'll ask Clarice to make you my understudy," I offer.

"No way. I like dancing in the back. If I screw up, no one sees. You have nowhere to hide as a principal."

"Thank you so much."

Ida hugs me again. "*You* have nothing to worry about. See you at rehearsal." She kisses my cheek and runs off to her car, carefree.

I return to my own car and sit thoughtfully after I start it up. I briefly consider running away, but I pull out of the parking lot and drive resolutely back toward McLaughlin Renovations.

Who am I fooling? I'll always go back.

Ben will be there. I can't wait to see him again.

———

Ben

THAT WEEK, I GET TO KNOW ERIN.

We have lunch together each day after Monday, grabbing a bite at a local place. We talk. I'm not a talker, but with Erin, I find myself opening up.

I tell her what it's like to be the McLaughlin brother who isn't into sports and who learned machine language at age twelve. I could insult my brothers in binary code, and loved it when they had no idea what I was saying.

I'm tight with my brothers though, and I tell her about that too. How Zach and Ryan would be right there when bullies messed with me, and how they taught me to fight back. How we'd protect Austin too, the baby of the family, though his defense was his smart mouth and quick comebacks.

Erin tells me how she'd wanted to be a dancer since she was a little girl and her mother signed her up for lessons at the local Y. How she's fallen in love with dance and doesn't want to do anything else. She majored in dance performance in college, and then tried out for every dance company in the state and across the western U.S.

Reuben had seen her dance in a performance at the university, introduced himself backstage, and suggested she give Clarice a call. That's how she joined the West Valley Dance Company.

"I should be grateful to him," Erin says as we finish our sandwiches on Wednesday. "He was really nice to me at first. But ..."

"You don't have to talk about him," I tell her quickly. "In fact, I'd prefer it if you didn't."

"I want to explain." Erin's eyes are soft. "I don't think I was ever in love with him. Excited to be doing what I'd always dreamed of, and thankful he'd helped me. But it is over. O-V-E-R. Reuben promised what we had was forever, then he was gone."

"He's an asshole," I say in disgust. "You're better off without him."

"I realized that the day I woke up alone. It was like I could breathe again."

Erin flashes a smile. I smile with her, but I'm a little bummed. Does she mean she never wants to be stifled with a serious relationship?

Because that's what I have in mind, a relationship. I crumple the sandwich wrapping to keep from having to respond. I'll have to figure out how to introduce the idea without scaring her off.

———

I CONSULT WITH MY BROTHERS. AUSTIN HAS GIVEN me some good advice, but I approach Ryan for more. I avoid Zach, because he knows me too well. Zach, who is now goopy in love with Abby, will try to march me straight to Erin and make me go down on one knee.

But Erin's been burned. I want to gain her trust, not terrify her.

"A grand gesture," Ryan tells me when I corner him in his office. I pretend I'm in there to install an upgrade to one of his programs, and I hit him with my problem. "That's what women love. How do you think I finally got Calandra to say yes?"

"I remember us beating on you until you two got back together and figured things out."

Ryan flushes. Once he saw the light with Calandra, he became this enlightened guru on love and relationships. He's so full of shit.

"What kind of grand gesture?" I ask.

Ryan taps his fingers together and swivels his desk chair back and forth, like a detective about to wrap up a case.

"You have to tailor it to the woman. Make it something she can't resist."

"Stellar." I click the last button on the upgrade and drag the installer into the trash. "Your brilliant advice is that I'm on my own."

"Hey, love's a bitch. But it's also worth it."

Ryan, who used to glower every time anyone mentioned Calandra, beams like a ray of sunshine. Calandra announced she was pregnant a few weeks ago, and now Ryan is not only the love guru, but the expectant father one too. Like I said, full of shit.

On the other hand, I'm really happy for Ryan. He'd been a serious pain in the ass to live with when he and Calandra were going through their issues.

"Thanks, Ryan."

"Not a problem." Before I can get out of the room, he lands the bomb. "When are you going to tell Mom and Dad?"

"When I figure out where this is going. If it's going." I point at him. "Do *not* say a word."

Ryan crosses his heart. But his grin when I turn away is huge.

———

I PUT AUSTIN'S PLAN INTO MOTION FIRST.

"So," I say to Erin on Friday afternoon when the

business is starting to wind down. I'm behind her desk, again with the software updates—I've had to do so many this week. "Um ... I'm thinking about going out tonight. Want to come? If you, you know, don't have other plans."

Of course she'll have plans. She has friends, and her performances, though she told me they don't do the shows on Fridays. Saturday night and Sunday matinee is all, and in June, the season will be over.

Erin slides a pile of contracts neatly into a file drawer with her slim fingers. I love watching her handle paperwork.

"Okay." Her effortless response has my hopes rising. "What did you have in mind?"

Austin had suggested everything from a luxurious restaurant to staying home and watching a movie online—I would provide the pizza and snacks. *That way, if things start going well, the bedroom's only a few steps away.*

Austin thinks about only one thing. Not that I wasn't tempted to try it out.

I say the words in a rush. "How about we go dancing?"

Chapter Eight

Ben

ERIN STARES at me after I make my request, and I realize how lame the idea is. She dances all the time. Why would she want to do it on her down time?

I should have gone with the movie and snacks idea. Austin is better at this than I am.

Erin's smile flows across her face. "Okay. Sounds like fun."

I try not to make my relief obvious. "Great. I'll pick you up? Say seven?"

"I think clubs don't really get rolling until nine or later."

I've never been to a club, so how would I know?

"We can eat first," I say quickly.

"Even better."

"Good." But wait, there's more. It was easier to date when I was younger—no one had any money so we just hung out at whatever pizza or burger place was nearby. "Um ... where would you like to go?"

Erin's eyes crinkle behind her glasses. "Wherever is good for me. You pick the restaurant."

"Oh, sure, no pressure." If it sucks, it will bring down the evening before we start.

"How about ..." Erin scans the menus she collects so my brothers can decide where to take clients out to lunch. "This one. It seems fun."

It's part of a local chain, with easy-to-understand food and a patio. I read the menu, noticing the price range lies somewhere between cheap and stupidly expensive. "We can try it. If it's bad, we'll blame my brothers."

"It won't be bad. Looking forward to it."

My family begins to stream out of their offices, ready to hit their weekends. They all have plans. Ryan and Calandra will do what newlyweds do—curtain shopping or something, plus sex. Zach and Abby will do what engaged couples do—wedding planning and sex. Austin, probably just sex.

Austin pauses at the desk and taps the top of it with his fists. "Later, kids." He saunters out.

Erin finishes shutting down the office for the night. I do the same on my end. If any computer glitches occur over the weekend, guess who gets the whiny texts about it? I decide that if any glitch happens tonight, I'm ignoring it. Plenty of time to fix whatever in the morning.

Erin and I are the last to leave. She locks the door, like the responsible employee she is.

I walk her to her car. Since no one is around, parking lot empty, I kiss her lightly on the lips. "See you later."

"Yes, you will."

I love how jazzed I am as I get into my truck. She drives out first, me hanging back to see that she leaves safely. Then I crank up my sound system and sing along with T-Bone Walker, badly, at the top of my lungs all the way home.

———

THE RESTAURANT IS DECENT, WHICH I THINK relieves us both. We like it enough that we tentatively say we'll come back. Together.

We hit the club and that's when things change. What was I thinking? This is Austin's kind of place, seriously out of my comfort zone. Erin looks apprehensive as we walk in, and I say bad things about my brother in my head.

The club is jammed. It's cavernous, with a high ceiling. Bright lights shine on the dance floor, where bodies gyrate up and down. The floor is ringed with tables on three shallow tiers, receding into darkness, with a bar snaking along one of the side walls.

It looks like people come here in packs, clusters of girls together or a mix of men and women. There aren't many couples alone.

I hold tightly to Erin's hand as we make our way to the bar, afraid I'll lose her. She might go down in the sea of people, and I'll never find her again.

Erin keeps it simple with wine, and I go for an even simpler beer. Now to find a place to sit while we drink. The pounding music makes it impossible for us to discuss where we want to go—we mouth and use hand signals.

Ten minutes later, we luck out with a table in a corner on the upper tier as a party leaves. A harried waitress gives it a sloppy wipe down, and we sit.

"We can't ever get up and dance," I shout to Erin over the music. "Someone will snag the table." Probably why everyone arrives in groups. There'll always be someone to save the spot.

"We'll guard it for you." A woman at the next table, who is planted firmly on her boyfriend's lap, offers this with a big smile. The boyfriend, who has his hand on her thigh under her skirt, pays no attention. Their friends, another couple, are thoroughly kissing each other.

"Thanks," Erin says. "Appreciate it."

The other woman waves off the thanks and nuzzles her boyfriend.

Erin regards the dance floor in longing, one foot tapping to the thumping beat. My worry that she'll be unhappy with my choice of outing fades. But there's another problem.

"I can't actually dance," I call across the table.

"Zach tried to teach me, but he gave up. Said it was hopeless."

"Zach isn't me."

"What?" I lean toward her, not sure I heard her right.

"I said, Zach isn't me. I'll teach you. I've taught four-year-olds. You can't be much harder."

I want to laugh. "Sure, I can."

Erin pops out of her seat, drink forgotten. "Come on."

She grabs me by the hand and leads me from our hard-won table, down the tiers and to the dance floor.

I don't recognize the music playing. Something with a fast beat, computerized voice modulators, and instrument simulation. I know *how* it's created, but I've never heard the song.

Erin and I squeeze onto the floor. Lots of dancing going on—groups, couples, women dancing together. Erin and I find a relatively open spot with some difficulty.

She puts her hands on my shoulders and sways into me. Not the best way to get me to move—my feet are frozen to the floor. I want to savor the moment with Erin, not shake my body. I'll look like an idiot anyway.

Erin proves her dance knowledge goes well beyond ballet. She finds the beat and slides her body in effort-less moves. She becomes the music, first flowing, then rocking, hips, arms, and legs moving in perfect time.

She catches the attention of those around us. They gravitate toward her, naturally attracted. I kind of shuffle my feet and pretend to dance, but no one is fooled.

"She's outta your league, dude," a guy informs me. He wants me to fade so he can dance with Erin.

Screw that. I move closer to her. Erin lays her arms on my shoulders and rocks against me.

"See? Can't dance." I canter back and forth, way off the beat. "These guys will lynch me to be with you."

"No." Erin shakes her head. She takes off her glasses and stuffs them in the little bag she carries on her wrist. "I'll show you what to do—Dean does a lot of standing while I work."

She wrinkles her nose as she confides this, as though pleading with me not to tell Dean she just said that.

"Dean seems like he knows what he's doing even standing still," I say. "Not me."

"Don't worry. I'll make you look good."

Erin spins around once, and I realize from the sudden gleam in her eye that she was just getting warmed up.

The song changes to a new one, but to me it's essentially the same, only a little slower. Similar wavering female voice, booming under-beat, and synthesized lead instruments.

The slightly slower tempo makes Erin's moves more sensual. She can take her time with her hip sways, her graceful arms, and her body swishing against mine and away. I'm afraid to move, because I don't want the whole club seeing I'm getting hard for her. Desire can be so inconvenient.

Erin rests her hand on my shoulder as she kicks her leg out, her skirt swinging. She arches back and then slides around me like a harem dancer in an old movie.

People are watching, admiring, envying. Erin moves against me in beautiful waves, her entire body feeling the music.

She places my arm around her waist, then shows me how to toss her from one half embrace to the other arm. Erin falls against me then pivots and falls again, as though gravity will take her at any moment. But I feel her strength, her perfect sense of balance that betrays how much control she has.

I'm proud of myself for figuring out the move, but Erin isn't finished. She tells me in my ear to lift her under her hips, and I scoop her up with one arm. She positions herself, which helps me shift my weight to do it right.

I spin around with her. She's half sitting on my arm, half holding on to me. The picture she makes is a graceful curve around my body, as beautiful as anything she and Dean do together on stage.

Around and around we go, me getting slightly dizzy, but Erin never wavers.

The song winds down as we glide in a wide circle like ice dancers. We have room because the crowd has backed off, watching us in awe.

"Slower." Erin's voice warms my ear. "End with the song."

I don't know when the song's going to finish, but finally, the beats peter out, and the woman singer finishes with a whisper: *I want to be with you, tonight.*

Erin and I halt, me on one knee, Erin draped against my torso. She cups my face with one hand, gazing down into my eyes.

The dancers in the club whoop, amazed and happy with our performance.

Erin smiles as she nuzzles my nose, and fire takes me. There has never been a more perfect moment—outside of bed with Erin—than this one.

I decide to make it even more perfect. I brush her cheek with my thumb, gently pull her close, and kiss her.

Erin's lips are soft, her breath hot from dancing. She kisses me with abandon, wrapping her arms around me.

The crowd cheers again, long *wooo's* coming from the guys. *Eat your hearts out, fellas.*

Another song begins. I barely hear it. I have Erin kissing me, and we're together like it's the most natural thing in the world.

Erin lifts her head and brushes a kiss across the bridge of my nose. She looks into the throng around us, and abruptly freezes.

"Oh, shit," she whispers.

I stand up and assist her to her feet, though she's steadier than I am. I glance to where she's staring, and understand her alarm.

At the edge of the group, eyes fixed on us, are my

brothers. Ryan, Zach, Austin. With Ryan and Zach are Calandra and Abby. Austin is alone, and he's the only one laughing his butt off.

Standing beside my brothers are, unbelievably, my mom and dad. Here. In a club in downtown Phoenix, on a Friday night.

Erin starts to tear her hand from mine, but I don't let go. There's nothing we can do now.

The secret is out. My whole family has seen me kissing Erin, and now we find out what kind of shit will hit the fan.

Chapter Nine

Erin

THE ENTIRE MCLAUGHLIN family has just witnessed me kissing the hell out of Ben.

I scan their faces—what are they even doing here?—and find mixed reactions. Austin is grinning as though he's not a bit surprised. Ryan's not surprised either, but he's glancing at his parents as though worried about their response.

Zach is amazed. His mouth is open, his eyes wide, and he'd look comical if I wasn't so mortified.

Abby, next to him, is beaming at me. She gives me a fist pump. I don't know Calandra well, but she appears happy with me too.

Now for the McLaughlin parents, the people I actually work for. Mr. McLaughlin—Alan—regards us thoughtfully. I can't tell what he thinks. Virginia does not look pleased. Not outraged or shocked or anything. She's ... disappointed?

"Holy crap." I try again to wrest my hand from Ben's, but his grip is tight. "I'm outta here. It was nice working for you all."

"No way." Ben tugs me closer. "They saw. They can suck it up. They'll like you better if you don't run."

I know that's true. I'm not usually such a coward. But now I have to look Virginia McLaughlin in the eye and admit that, yeah, I'm sleeping with her son.

We don't have much choice about fleeing anyway. McLaughlins surge around us, three brothers, Abby and Calandra, and the parents. Austin is the first to reach us. He winks at me and slings an arm around Ben.

"Nice dancing, bro. Didn't know you had it in you."

"I don't," Ben says. "It was all Erin."

"I saw that." Austin gives me a thumbs-up. He lets Ben go to put his arm around me. "Chin up," he says in my ear. "Mom's scary, but she's got a good heart."

"Thanks," I mutter. "Wait a minute. Why don't you seem surprised? Ben, did you tell him ..."

"Nope." Austin cuts in quickly to save his brother. "I guessed. Plus, Ben asked me for a good place to take you out. I said this club. Am I right?" He waves his arm at the room like a proud parent.

"This was *your* idea?" I'm not sure whether to be angry or laugh. "Well, it was ... actually, this was wonderful. Thanks, Ben."

Ben, who's been watching Austin warily, blows out a breath. "I felt stupid asking a dancer to go dancing."

"No, it's perfect. I love to dance. It's nice to do it for fun, no pressure."

Until now, with his family bearing down on us. Austin and Ben remain on either side of me, a buffer against the rest of them. Abby tells me they have a big table on the first tier, and invites us to join them. Zach, recovering his shock, rushes off to get us fresh drinks.

I'm not sure how it happens, but I find myself seated next to Virginia. She's watching me with eyes the same color as Ben's, though Ben overall looks more like his father.

I decide to confront her head on. "If you want me to quit, I will." I lift the glass of wine Zach has just set down in front of me. "But I'm not sorry I'm going out with Ben. I really like him."

"Why should you quit?" Virginia asks. Her drink is a blood red wine, same as mine. "I need your help."

I'm relieved she hasn't instantly demanded I stay away from Ben, but I'm a little confused. "If it's awkward," I try.

Ben is next to me, his arm around me, but he's fending off questions from Zach on his other side.

"It doesn't need to be awkward." Virginia has a piercing gaze. "But I wish I'd known. You don't have to sneak around, you know. I really like Ben too."

Alan leans around her, his expression kind. "She's only mad because you didn't tell her right away. Ginny *hates* being surprised."

"I don't hate to be surprised ..." Virginia begins.

"I threw her a surprise party for her fiftieth birthday, and I thought she'd blow a gasket." Alan lifts his hands. "Never again."

"I wasn't mad. It was a wonderful party." Virginia sips wine, as though realizing she's losing control of the conversation. "I was just ... surprised."

"You should have heard her language. I don't think our friends ever laughed so hard."

"Are you talking about Mom's surprise party?" Ryan leans over. "Yeah, that was something."

"Will you stop going on about the party?" Virginia demands. "This concerns Erin and Ben."

Alan pats her hand. "I think they have things figured out. Abby and Zach work fine in the same office. Erin and Ben will too. They have so far."

"I'm not angry at—"

Alan doesn't let her finish. "Come on, let's dance. I need to shake it. The music is calling."

Virginia shoots me an appealing look, as though begging me to save her, but I decide to sit back and smile. Alan tugs her up. Virginia releases her wine glass at the last moment and lets her husband tow her to the dance floor.

Austin slides to take Virginia's seat, watching his parents. "Do I want to see this?"

"Of course you do," Abby says across the table. "It's sweet."

"Bleh." Austin shudders.

Ben takes my hand. "You okay?"

"I think so." I let out a breath. "Your mom is scary. Especially since I work for her."

"We all work for her," Ben reminds me. "Don't worry. She likes you."

I'm starting to feel better. Virginia didn't glare me down and fire me on the spot, and the others seem to be okay with me sticking my tongue down Ben's throat. Zach has lost his dumbfounded expression and is smiling at us now.

"Wow." Austin continues to watch Virginia and Alan, who are on the dance floor, Alan holding one of Virginia's hands. They spin and sway, perfectly at home with the music. "Hey, who knew Dad could boogie?"

"I did," Ben says. "Mom and Dad dance all the time. They did competitions when they were in college."

"Seriously?" Austin leans back with his drink. "How do you know this and I don't?"

"I pay attention when they talk." Ben relaxes, his arm resting on the back of my chair.

I like the feeling so much, I snuggle into him. Austin's eyes glint, but what the hell? They know. Now to find out if they think me a temp girlfriend, like in my job, or what I hope—that this happiness I've found with Ben will last.

———

BEN DRIVES ME HOME. "GOOD NIGHT," HE SAYS when he pulls into my driveway.

He's not turning cold—I understand he's trying to be nice. Worried I'm upset about his family descending on us and thinking I might want to be alone. He's already told Austin he's a dead man for bringing them all there. Austin looked cheerful about that.

Virginia was much happier by the end of the night. Dancing with her husband, surrounded by her kids, a grandchild on the way ... I think she decided that me and Ben snogging on the dance floor was not so bad in the grand scheme of things.

Maybe that's what Austin was trying to show her. I won't let Ben kill him, in that case.

I reach over and take Ben's hand. "Stay," I say softly.

His grin flashes, the crooked one I'm growing to love. Ben sets the brake, turns off the truck, and kisses me.

We steam up the windows by the time we're done. Then Ben hops out, dashes around to my side, and escorts me from the pickup. We dart inside the house— no dropping my keys this time—kiss frantically once the door is closed, and make our hurried way to the bedroom.

———

IDA HAD BEEN RIGHT THAT CLARICE WOULDN'T pair me with Reuben. All week, he dances with the *corps de ballet* in a secondary male part Clarice invents for him. Dean and I rehearse separately from them.

When I peek inside the large practice room at Clarice's studio, I have to admit Reuben is good. He picks up the steps quickly and even helps those who are in the scene with him without losing patience.

He could be like that, nice to the point of donating a kidney. Before, I'd thought him a wonderful human being. Now I have to wonder what he's up to.

When I reach the theater Saturday, with Ben, Reuben is even apologetic.

"Sorry I went off on you," he says to Ben. Reuben's face is half made up, his skin powdered and rouged, lips outlined. A paper bib protects his shirt. "I confess, I was crazy about Erin. You can see why. But hey, I had my shot. Now it's your turn."

Ben's obviously not buying the contrite act, but Reuben doesn't notice and rushes away to finish dressing. Dean, already in full face paint, risks wrinkling his thick eyeliner by scrunching up his face.

"Kiss-ass," he says in Reuben's direction. "How are you, Ben?"

"Just fine."

Dean looks him up and down. "I can see that. You're glowing. Erin's good for you." He pauses thoughtfully. "You're good for her."

I have to get into costume, so I kiss Ben quickly and slip away, trying not to blush at Dean's assessment. Dean, instead of making for the warm-up area, holds back to speak to Ben. They're getting along well, those two.

The performance tonight is excellent, all of us on peak. Reuben is really good, I have to admit, injecting an energy into the part of the show that had needed something more.

Dean, who will never let any male dancer upstage him, does better than usual. Competition brings out the best in him. He also gives fair dues, and when Reuben gets great applause, Dean brings him to the front with us and we all three take a bow.

Afterward, Reuben remains cordial, congratulating everyone on a good show.

When Ben comes backstage, Reuben gives him a friendly greeting and disappears into his dressing room.

I still don't trust him.

Ben takes me home. And he stays. This time, he's brought an overnight bag and has stocked up from the drugstore. At the rate we're blowing through condoms, we'll need reserves.

As I lay next to him, trying to catch my breath after an intense round of lovemaking, I wonder where this is going.

Should I worry about it? Or simply enjoy what I have? Ben and I might not last together—the future is always uncertain. Being with Reuben taught me that.

My thoughts scatter when Ben rolls onto his side and softly kisses me. The kisses grow stronger, Ben's hands bringing my body to life.

Before we go further, we clean up with a shower,

which involves more kissing, caressing, sliding soap in all the right places. When we return to the bed, I push him down onto it and climb on top of him. He's surprised, but doesn't argue when I straddle him, lowering myself onto his waiting cock.

It's wonderful rocking on him while he cups my breasts and smiles up at me, his eyes dark and soft. I've done things with Ben I've never tried before, and my heart is full.

The next day is the Sunday matinee, where Reuben again performs well, and the show is a hit.

When I hop into Ben's truck afterwards, he hesitates before he turns on the ignition. "I've been instructed to show up at the folks' house for Sunday dinner," he says, sounding apologetic. "I'm supposed to bring you. But if you'd rather go home, I'll drop you there. I won't inflict my family on you if you don't want to see them right now."

My heart sinks, but I force a smile. "No, it's fine. We can go."

Ben's brows rise. "You sure?"

I shrug. "I'll have to face them sooner or later. Better now, with food and wine to make everyone mellow, than on Monday morning before coffee."

He watches me another moment, then starts the pickup. "All right. But anytime you want out of there, tell me and we'll leave."

"It will be okay." If I say it often enough, I'll believe it.

We arrive at the house, Ben holding my hand as we

walk in. We're immediately intercepted by Calandra and Abby, Zach behind them.

"We need to talk wedding plans," Abby sings to me.

Zach claps Ben on the shoulder. "Run," he says to Ben. "Trust me."

Ben clearly doesn't want to leave us, but Calandra and Abby promise to take good care of me, and Ben finally lets Zach lead him off.

The ladies take me to the corner of the backyard where a bar has been set up, and Abby thrusts a glass of wine into my hand. Calandra is drinking water but doesn't seem unhappy about it.

"First order of business," Abby says. She points at me. "You, my bridesmaid. Is that okay with you?"

I smile with genuine pleasure. "I'd love to. Thank you."

"Good. I wanted to ask you before, but I wasn't sure you'd be interested. But now that you're with Ben … you're family. You can't say no." Abby beams at me and sips her wine.

I take a gulp. "I'm *sort of* with Ben. We haven't, you know, discussed a relationship. It was just a—"

"One-night stand?" Calandra finishes, and Abby chuckles. "A pretty long one-night stand, I'm guessing. Same thing happened to me with Ryan. And Abby with Zach."

"A long one-night stand?" I ask in puzzled amusement. "What is that?"

"It's when you have one beautiful night together—and he doesn't leave," Abby answers. "And you don't leave either. Next thing you know, you're standing in the McLaughlin backyard asking your friends to be your bridesmaids."

My face grows hot, and I wave my glass. "Whoa. No weddings. We've only been seeing each other a week."

"And pining for each other a long time before that," Calandra says. "Don't worry," she adds with confidence. "You're together."

I know they're trying to be nice, but I don't want to discuss it—this is between Ben and me, and it's too new, too tender. I derail the conversation by asking Abby how the wedding plans are going.

That's good for nearly an hour of talk, Abby excited about what's right and frustrated about what's wrong. No wedding ever comes off without a glitch or two.

Ben returns to escort me as we troop into dinner. I've attended the McLaughlin Sunday get-togethers before and usually enjoy them. Virginia doesn't cook the meal herself—she's busy and picks up ready-made food from grocery stores. But Alan grills, with Ryan's help, and the rest of us throw stuff together in the kitchen. Between the family, it all gets on the table, and we sit down to eat.

Ben makes sure I'm next to him. Austin slides in on my other side before anyone else can.

"Don't worry," he whispers. "I'm here to fend off embarrassing questions you might be pestered with."

He and Ben protect me from the others who clearly want to probe for details about what Ben and I have going on. Austin is good at interrupting any question that starts off too eagerly, or loudly asking for food to be passed if he senses I'm uncomfortable.

Ben, unworried, easily parries his brothers' teasing by giving back as good as they give him. Somehow he and Austin make sure that no one asks about our sex life, or where we're going with our relationship, or if we're moving in together.

After supper, we break into teams for board games, boys against girls. Alan softly plays piano in the background.

At one point, Abby casually tells Austin, "I saw Brooke the other day."

His instant tension speaks volumes. "Oh?"

"Yeah, she looked great. She said to tell you hi."

Austin gives her a frown. "Are you sure she didn't say *tell him to go to hell?*"

"Nope." Abby smiles. "She said hello. That's all."

Austin shudders and returns to his after-dinner coffee.

We play Trivial Pursuit and Pictionary, and the girls trump the boys. Virginia is especially good at both, and I'm happy she's on my side.

I also like the way she looks over at Alan from time to time, the love in her eyes plain. There's a reason the McLaughlins are a close family. They love unashamedly.

By the end of the night, it's obvious I've been accepted into their circle. I've been invited to their parties before, but tonight they've embraced me.

It makes me happy, and I sigh with contentment as Ben and I walk out in the cool darkness. He kisses me before he tucks me into his truck and we drive back to my house.

I'm pleased the McLaughlins like me, but it's a little scary too. If Ben and I fall apart, as has happened in every other relationship I've been in, losing the family will be extra hurt on top.

————

MONDAY MORNING I WALK INTO THE OFFICE WITH a lighter heart. Everyone says an extra friendly hello to me as they pass my desk.

Ben is a little late, because he went home to do laundry before coming in. He sends me a smile when he enters, and when no one's looking, he sneaks behind my desk and gives me a long kiss.

Things are going well, the family cheerful as we settle down to business. Abby keeps shooting me *we need to talk* signals, but in a good way.

Yes, everything is fantastic in my world, until after lunch, when Reuben walks in.

I launch myself from my chair. "What are you doing here?" I keep my voice low, but it's vehement.

Reuben blinks, his dark gaze taking in the showroom and then me. I used to think his eyes soulful. Now I'm reminded of a cow.

"Is this how you greet all your customers?" he asks.

"You're not a customer," I snap. "You don't need anything renovated."

"That's true. I like rentals. So freeing." Reuben leans on my counter, and the smile he sends me is genial, nothing more. "Actually, I came to talk to Ben."

"Ben?" I give him a level stare. "Why?"

"Erin, you are so suspicious. Though I can't blame you, I suppose. I was selfish, and I know it. Can't we let bygones be bygones?"

"I'd love to, if I knew the real reason you moved back to Phoenix."

I expect him to stammer an excuse, but Reuben smiles again. "The real reason is I need more experience. It's why I begged Clarice to take me back. I was out of my league up north and I knew it."

That sounds logical, but I'm surprised Reuben admits it.

I'm about to grill him on why he wants to talk to Ben, when Ben himself comes barreling out of his office.

"What do you need?" Ben moves to my desk, ready to shove himself between me and Reuben.

"Hello, Ben." Reuben greets him with a friendly nod. "Can I take up a few minutes of your time? I know I don't deserve it, but I promise I won't keep you long. I need to ask you something."

Ben glances at me, and I shrug, spreading my hands. I have no idea what it's about.

I'm hoping Ben decides to throw Reuben out the door, maybe calling on Zach, Ryan, and Austin to assist, but Ben silently gestures Reuben to precede him. Ben takes him, not to his office, but outside to the parking lot.

The two start walking, making a circuit of the building. I strain to keep them in view as long as I can, but they're soon around the windowless side and gone, leaving me stewing and worried.

Chapter Ten

Ben

AFTER ABOUT TWENTY minutes of conversation, Reuben says his goodbyes, climbs into his car, and takes off.

He's left me ... what's the word? Dumbfounded.

When I return to the office, Erin charges around her desk to me. "What did he want?"

"Well ..." I'm not sure how to begin.

Her eyes are wide, glasses glinting under the skylights. "Damn it, Ben, don't do the suspense thing. Did he challenge you to a duel?"

I stare at her in amazement before I bust up laughing. She's not serious, but I can imagine Reuben doing it.

"Can you take a break?" I ask.

Erin zips behind her desk, clicks something on her

computer, and switches off her hands-free phone with rapidity. I lead her to my office.

Stacks of humming computers and a shelf of cords and computer parts adorn the room. My desk is clean and neat, only my desktop computer on it. My brothers always seem to have papers everywhere, but I don't have a scrap in sight. Drives my mom crazy whenever she wants to leave me a note.

Erin has been in here before—she's told me the room went with me, whatever that meant. Today, she's too impatient to look around.

"Ben, I'm so sorry." Erin clasps her fingers loosely in front of her. "Reuben has no right to bother you, no right to bother *anyone*."

"Hey." I take her hands—I have to pry them apart. "Reuben's not your fault. He's an asshole all by himself."

That wins a little smile. "What did he say?"

I mull over the weird conversation I'd had with Reuben. We'd slowly circled the parking lot as we talked, shaded by mesquites and thick oleanders that separate our business from the one next door.

"He wanted to reassure me he hasn't come back for you," I tell her. "That he knows he screwed up with you. He's happy you've found someone new, and will bow out gracefully."

Erin scowls. "He has a big ego."

"Yeah, that's obvious." I squeeze her hands. "Like it's up to him who you go out with. But he seemed sincere." I frown, still pondering. "It was strange. I kept trying to get mad at him, but then Reuben would deflect that and be contrite. He apologized a lot. Like he was losing sleep over his behavior and wouldn't be absolved until he came and talked to me."

"Hmm." Erin swings our entwined hands, and I find myself wanting to move closer. "Maybe he has reformed for real. I doubt it, but you never know. He might have had an epiphany." She pins me with her gaze. "Does not mean I'm interested in him."

She sounds worried I won't believe her. I can't help bending to her and giving her a kiss.

The kiss could have changed into something more serious, but Erin eases back. "Is that really all he wanted?"

I have to shake my head. "He wants to dance with you in the show. A *pas de* whatever-it's-called. Wanted to assure me it was purely professional. He says you're one of the best dancers he's ever met, and you can help him grow. His words. He wanted my blessing."

Erin stares at me in perplexity and growing anger. "He asked *you*? Why the hell didn't he ask *me*? The idiot. Or discuss it with Clarice? And Dean? If we add a *pas de deux* to this show, we'll have to cut or trim one of mine with Dean, who will not be happy."

I squeeze her hands again, pulling her back to the here and now. "I told Reuben he should be talking to you instead of me. But he said he was afraid to approach you directly, knowing you'd say no. I think he wants me to persuade you."

"The total jerk." She's fuming now, cheeks flushed.

"He's not wrong about you being a good dancer." I picture how she glides across the stage in perfect elegance.

Erin isn't soothed. "He's changed his tune. Reuben used to criticize me all the time, like I wasn't good enough to dance with *him*. I wonder what the hell happened to him in Milwaukee."

"He got cold?" I glance out my slit of a window at the blazing May sunshine. "I hear they have winter there."

"Ha ha," Erin says, straight-faced. "You think I should agree?"

"What?" I pull my brain back from fantasies of Erin dancing like a goddess, except naked in her bedroom, just for me. "No, I'm just telling you what he said—it was a bizarre conversation." I stand closer, moving my hands to cup her elbows. "It's your life, your career, your choice. I'd never tell you to do what *I* want, or talk you into going against your gut."

Erin's eyes go rounder. "Wow. That's the nicest thing any guy has ever said to me."

"Really?" The corners of my mouth twitch. "That's kind of sad."

"Reuben is right though, that any interaction I have with him now is purely professional. I am truly over him. I don't want you to worry about ..."

I touch Erin's face, and her words trail off. The fact that she's reassuring me she won't dump me for a good-looking, well-built guy the ladies in the audience drool over is the nicest thing any woman has said to *me*.

"Erin." I brush my thumb across her cheekbone. "I'm not worried about you. You're awesome. Kind and sweet, and not the type to string along two guys at once. You're true. It's one of the things I love about you."

She stills, her eyes fixed on mine, lips parted. A few heartbeats go by.

Then I realize I've just said the *L-* word.

Damn it—I was supposed to save that for the grand gesture. Oh, well, I screw up stuff like this all the time. Falling in love isn't the same as setting up an efficiently elegant, bug-free program.

Love has lots of bugs in it. I'm figuring that out.

Erin drags in a long breath, and then she launches herself at me. Her arms are around me, and we're kissing and kissing.

We fall to the non-static floor mat, which is soft, our legs tangling as we devour each other. My hand is on her breast, hers running down my back to grip my ass.

"Hey, Ben, could you help me with—" Austin's voice breaks off, and we hear his startled exclamation, followed by quickly retreating footsteps. His voice trails behind him. "Aw, man. This place is *not* safe for work anymore."

———

Erin

AFTER A LONG AFTERNOON OF THOUGHT, I RELENT and tell Clarice I'm fine doing a *pas* with Reuben, but

Dean has final say. I suggest it needs a meeting with me, Dean, Clarice, and Reuben to discuss it all before making decisions, which is how Reuben should have handled it in the first place.

Not going behind our backs and asking my boyfriend's permission, the git.

Clarice agrees and we fix a time to meet during rehearsals tonight.

On the other hand ...

Ben's words, *It's one of the things I love about you,* continue to ring in my head. Reuben's visit caused the phrase to slip from Ben's mouth, and I'm almost grateful to Reuben for that. Ben got embarrassed as soon as he said the words, and I kissed the hell out of him before he could take it back.

Good thing Austin had come in, or we *both* might have been fired.

I hug the feeling to myself that evening in Clarices's office at her studio as Reuben tries to convince Dean and Clarice he needs to dance with me. Neither Clarice, Dean, nor I are sure of his motives, but I'm in a great mood.

"Sure," I say. "We can do something short. We wouldn't have to cut any of my dances with Dean that way."

Dean gives me an amazed look, opens his mouth to argue, then shuts it again. Clarice has the final word—it's her show—and she takes a moment to consider.

Clarice is in her sixties, with very short gray hair and a willowy dancer's body. She still performs for the fun of it and she choreographs and teaches us all the dances herself.

She purses her pink-lipsticked mouth while she thinks. "All right. I don't want to hide you in the chorus anyway, Reuben. The audience likes you, so you can have a few minutes in the front with Erin. Actually I'm having an idea for a *pas de trois* as well." She sends Reuben a sudden frown. "But no ad libbing. You do my steps and don't mess up my show."

Reuben lifts his hands in surrender. "Thank you. I promise you, Erin, this is purely dance. And, Dean, I'm not trying to upstage you. Like anyone could."

He delivers the last words with a twist of lips that makes it a possible insult. That's more Reuben's style.

Dean chooses to ignore the poke at his ego. "All right. We'll need extra time to learn all this, which means you're paying for dinner, Reuben."

Reuben rolls his eyes. Clarice dismisses us, and we head to the studio's large mirrored rehearsal room.

I hang back with Dean. "You gave in easily," I remark.

Dean shrugs, glancing at Reuben, who is yards down the hall from us already, eager to begin.

"Keeps him from whining. Clarice will turn his demands into an asset—we all know that."

"Hmm." I study Dean closely, and he mouths, *What?* "You're getting mellow in your thirties," I say. "Feeling all right?"

Dean puffs up in mockery of his own usual attitude. "I'm perfectly fine. If I'm mellow it's because I'm happy for you. I'm just a romantic at heart, I guess."

"What does that mean?" I ask, perplexed. He was hiding something.

"Nothing." Dean takes my hand and rushes me down the hall. "Let's learn this new stuff. Time's a wasting."

I let him tow me into the rehearsal room. Clarice joins us and we start working out the logistics.

It's one of the things I love about you.

I hug the words to myself. I'm a romantic at heart too.

———

IT'S SATURDAY NIGHT. THE SHOW IS GOING WELL, as are the additional dances we've added. Clarice has kept them short, and we'll grow them as the performances continue.

True to his word, Reuben has not pestered me all week, only discussing dance when we converse. No mention of our past, our relationship, his departure, his return, or our present circumstances. If Ben comes up in conversation—both Ida and Dean make sure to mention him as often as possible—Reuben either remains neutral or says, "He's a decent guy."

I'm puzzled, but relieved.

Tonight we're debuting the new additions. Dean, Reuben, and I do a *pas de trois* in the first act, me going back and forth between them—like a dancing three-way. My character is apparently torn between the two guys, though she picks Dean in the end. Smart lady.

The audience loves it. They applaud us and some even rise when we're finished to show their appreciation.

I'm pleased, but also very nervous tonight. Joining Ben in the second row is his entire family. The four brothers, Alan and Virginia, Abby and Calandra, a few cousins from the extended family, and Great Aunt Mary. She's dating someone now, the very good-looking silver fox next to her. Go Aunt Mary.

Whenever I happen to glance into the audience, which I try not to do, I see faces of McLaughlins. I focus on Ben, make myself relax, and dance with renewed vigor.

Before the intermission, Reuben and I do a brief *pas de deux*. It's a "farewell" dance, where our characters are putting our pasts behind us and parting, so my lady can return to Dean. Very fitting. Clarice is a canny woman.

Reuben dances well, better than I've ever witnessed him do. He never misses a step, his *entrechat* —jumping up straight and switching his feet back and forth in midair—makes him look light and floating, as though gravity doesn't apply to him. Whenever he has to catch me, he does it without a slip. He holds me like a rock for my deep arabesques, and his spins are fast and perfect.

We finish with what's called a fish dive—both my legs point back up in the air, with my chest forward and my arm extended to the floor, while Reuben supports me via his thigh and arm with seeming effortlessness.

It's an elegant pose, and a trusting one. If he drops me, I'll land flat on my face and possibly be injured.

We pull it off without a hitch, thus ending the first half of the show.

The crowd explodes into a standing ovation. Reuben takes his bows without apology, and he gestures to me, giving me full dues. The applause comes on even stronger.

When the curtain closes, Reuben drops my hand and bolts from the stage. I follow more slowly to catch my breath. I need to keep my energy high for the second half.

I find Reuben in the hall behind the stage talking to guys in suits I don't recognize. They have dancers' builds, but I can tell they stopped dancing a while ago. Probably are ballet connoisseurs now.

Ben enters from the stage wings, and I smile at him. My heart always lightens when I see him coming.

"Here's Erin," Reuben is saying.

The men in suits turn to me. Reuben is smiling like a maniac, and the men greet me with interest.

"Your talent is amazing," one says to me. "Congratulations. Have you thought about taking it to a larger company? Say in Los Angeles?"

"Not really," I say. "I like dancing with Clarice."

Reuben grabs my hand and pulls me to his side, ignoring Ben. "She's modest, I told you."

"Well, you two make an awesome pair," says the

second guy. "Reuben is trying to convince us to extend the offer to you, and we told him we'd have to see you perform first. But wow. He's right."

"Offer?" I shake free of Reuben and move to Ben, who's beside me like a rock.

The suits look blank. "He didn't tell you?" asks the first guy.

"Wanted it to be a surprise," Reuben says to me quickly. "So you wouldn't be disappointed if they weren't interested."

Ben rumbles from beside me, "Disappointed about what?"

"We're recruiting Reuben," the second guy says. "Or trying to. He's got feelers out, he says, but we spotted him first." He sounds proud.

"Recruiting?" I glance from one face to the other— the two suit guys excited, Ben scowling, Dean, who is hovering on the edge of the conversation, furious, and Reuben, both triumphant and shamefaced.

The first suit pulls a card from his pocket and hands it to me. "This is us. We're not the biggest company in L.A., but we're well known and award-winning. All the best talent wants to dance with us. We've decided to sign Reuben, but you'd fit in well, Erin. Consider it."

The card reads *Giles Hutton, President, Central Los Angeles Premier Ballet.*

I stare at Reuben, the light dawning. "This is why you wanted to have a bigger part in the show ..."

Because he knew these guys were coming, knew

they had the potential to offer him a job. So he could kick the dust of Clarice's company off his feet, as he's always wanted to, after using it to make him look good.

It's why he's been so nice to me, why he sucked up to Ben to talk me in to dancing with him. Why he's been the model professional dancer all week. The smarmy varmint.

"You—"

Ben cuts me off. "That's great, man," he says to Reuben. "Congratulations."

I gape at him, and so does Dean.

"We're thrilled," second suit guy says. "Well, we'll leave you to get on with it. See you after the show, Barrow."

Reuben nods to them, shaking their hands. They shake my hand too, the second man squeezing it. "Think about it." He winks, then moves on.

The three of us are left with Reuben. We face him in silence, watching Reuben grow red under his makeup.

Reuben lifts his hands defensively. "Hey, I need the job. I'm not getting stuck in this hellhole the rest of my life."

Sounds much more like the Reuben I know.

Dean advances on him. "You little prick. You used Erin to make yourself look good—anyone who dances with her does. She knows how to make you shine. I should break your legs—then no more dancing for you, boyo."

Reuben takes a worried step back. Dean is about to follow, but Ben stops him.

"No. It's all good." Ben gives Dean a hard look, as if saying, *Work with me.* "I'm glad for you, Reuben. You go kick ass in L.A."

Reuben, preening at the sudden support, sends Dean a lofty glance. "I will. Now I have costume change. See you onstage."

"The shit ..." Dean begins as Reuben hurries away.

I've caught on to what Ben's doing, and I relax. "No, let him go," I say. "He's an asshole and a user and always will be, but if we go with it, then he'll be an asshole user *in another state.*"

"Damn straight," Ben says. He twines his fingers through mine.

Dean's face smooths out. "Ah, I get it." He points at Ben and chuckles. "You're crafty. Great. I'll go help him pack."

He takes off down the hall, leaving me relatively alone with Ben.

Ben turns to me, his gaze pinning me until my heart starts fluttering. "What?" I whisper.

He leans closer. "I want to kiss you. All over. And not stop."

"I'd smear my makeup on you," I say softly.

"Don't care." Ben releases my hand and takes a deliberate step back. "I should go. You still have half a show to do." He grins. "Make sure Dean doesn't trip Reuben up there."

"I will. I want him gone." I move to Ben and kiss his cheek, leaving a scarlet streak on it.

I want to say, *I love you, Ben,* but I turn away, running on light feet to my dressing room.

———

Ben

WHEN I RETURN TO MY SEAT, RYAN INFORMS ME I have a swipe of lipstick on my cheek, but I have more important things to care about right now. Ryan gives me a bolstering half-hug and lets me go, knowing what's to come.

It's show time.

Chapter Eleven

Ben

THE SECOND HALF of the performance passes without me noticing much of it. I've seen the show several times now, and I note more places where they've changed things to add Reuben.

Dean, I can tell, is pissed off at him. The dance where Dean's supposed to be aggressive to Reuben is believable. Reuben shrinks from him, and I don't think he's acting.

Mostly I'm only interested in Erin. She's gliding around the stage as though she's air itself. At one point she's on tiptoe, spinning and spinning, one leg bent then kicking out, bent then out. Austin elbows me.

"Doesn't she get dizzy?" he murmurs.

"She knows what she's doing," I growl at him.

"She's awesome." Austin's admiration softens my irritation.

She *is* awesome. Beautiful. Kind. Funny. Generous. I know I'm madly in love with her. Have been for a while.

The show ends with Erin's finale with Dean. They put everything they have into it tonight, and when Erin finishes with her graceful bow, the theater comes apart. Everyone's on their feet cheering her, Dean, the company, even Reuben. Dean brings out Clarice, who gets her own applause, and flowers are carried to the stage, including a bouquet from me and one from my family.

The curtain should be coming down, but Dean shakes his head at the guy who works the curtain, and it stays open.

That's my cue. As Erin shoots Dean a puzzled look, I leave my seat and push my way to the aisle.

Of my family, only Ryan knows what I'm doing. He gives me a thump on the back as I pass him. The rest of the family watches me in perplexity and some annoyance. I think I've stepped on Zach's toes.

Dean hurries on strong feet to the edge of the stage and escorts me up onto it. Erin gives us both a *what-the-hell?* stare. The rest of the dancers and Clarice pause, curious.

As I approach Erin, Dean makes a sharp signal to someone in the wings, and music begins to play out of the sound system. The audience, who are slowly filing out, turn back to the stage in surprise.

I take Erin's hands. The song playing is the one we'd danced to at the club, where she'd showed me how even a guy with two left feet could enjoy the music. I grin at her and start to move.

Erin resists at first, then she shakes her head in bemusement and starts to dance with me. We do the arm-to-arm thing where she floats from one side of me to the other, and we finish up with her spinning around me.

She cups my face as she had at the club, and I sink down on one knee.

The music fades, Dean signaling as we'd discussed. I remain on one knee, taking Erin's hands.

"You're beautiful," I tell her, then I raise my voice so it will carry to the back of the theater.

"Erin Dixon, will you marry me?"

Erin's mouth pops open. Her eyes are outlined in up-swooping strokes, her lips with the curves of a happy woodland creature. Her makeup wars with her real face, which is tight with shock.

The audience is holding its breath. Austin's "Whoa ..." becomes lost in the rustle of expectation.

Erin's hands are cold in mine, in spite of her pulse pounding against my fingers. Her chest moves rapidly, her breath fast.

She's going to say no. I swallow, my blood turning to ice. She'll withdraw, shake her head, and walk away, and that will be that.

Erin closes her mouth, then her lips part again.

"Yes," she whispers. Then, *"Yes!"* She shouts it loud.

As I nearly fall on my ass in relief, Erin is on my

lap, her arms flung around me. She kisses me fervently, no worry about smearing me with makeup now.

The cheering and applause surge as I hold Erin close, her body on mine. Our mouths meet in kisses that turn deep, intense. We're holding each other hard, ignoring the shrieks and happy cries from our family and friends.

The sounds become strangely muffled, and finally, Erin raises her head. The curtain has closed, turning the stage into a stuffy tent with a rosin-dotted floor and cardboard scenery.

Erin slides from my lap to her feet and holds my hands while I stand.

"I love you," I say to her.

Erin puts her arms around me again, resting her head on my shoulder. Tears streak her cheeks, becoming sooty puddles on her chin.

"I love *you*, Ben. I do so much."

I hold her, and nothing else matters.

As soon as we ease apart, knowing we have to leave the stage sometime, Dean is beside us.

"That was wonderful." He wipes his eyes. "Look, you made me cry like a big galoot."

I hold out my hand. "Thanks for your help." I'd had to recruit Dean, or I couldn't have pulled this off. He's kept the secret well.

Erin blinks, and Dean grabs me and squeezes me in a huge bear hug. As I gasp for breath, he releases me and seizes Erin in turn.

"Dean—" Erin's voice cuts off as Dean squashes

her, and she rocks when he lets her go. "You were in on this?"

"Sure." Dean grins. "The look on your face ..." His eyes screw up and he swipes at them with the back of his hand. "Here I go again. You two are coming to the after party—don't you dare try not to. Drinks are on me."

He charges down the hall, a force of nature. That's Dean.

I take Erin's hands again. "Thank you for not saying no."

"Are you kidding me?" Erin pulls me to her. "I think I need to show you how much I wouldn't say no."

I warm inside, my worries falling away. "Sounds like something I'll enjoy."

"Me too."

Clattering feet and voices let us know it will be a while before Erin and I can celebrate on our own. Falling in love and taking that love to til-death-us-do-part makes us a piece of something larger than ourselves.

"Here they come," I say, as my brothers, their ladies, and my parents surge toward us, my Great Aunt Mary's new guy escorting her up the stairs. "My family."

"My family too now," Erin says with a sunny smile. "Which is no bad thing."

They're around us, all talking at once. Ryan is smug —he's the one who helped me figure out the grand gesture. Mom has her arms outstretched, the happiest

I've ever seen her. Now she's hugging Erin like she'll never let go. Erin is passed around, and I lose track of her.

But it's all right. She'll be there when I need her. We are *us* now.

————

Erin

SOMEHOW WE MAKE IT THROUGH THE AFTER-PARTY and all the toasts, the McLaughlins coming along, no gathering complete without them. I talk, smile, and laugh until I'm exhausted.

Even Reuben is congratulatory. I'm still annoyed with him for using me—again—but that anger has been swallowed by my present happiness. Reuben acts contrite, and genuinely glad for Ben and me, but I'm relieved he'll once more be gone from my life.

Dean gets drunk off his ass and gives me a big kiss on the mouth. He tries to give Ben one too, but Ben manages to evade him. Dean laughs as though he's never had so much fun.

It's very late before Ben and I break away and head home. Virginia hugs me one more time before I go.

"Welcome to the family, honey," she says. "I'm so happy I could spit. But I won't." She pulls me aside and lowers her voice. "I meant to announce this tonight, as a surprise, but Ben upstaged me, so I'll just tell you. I called the temp agency on Friday and said I wanted you permanently—you'll now be working directly for us. That is, if you still want the job."

I stare at her in astonishment, then I do a spontaneous leap. "Yes!" I shout. My job is perfect—it's low-stress and lets me focus on dance, and I enjoy being part of the McLaughlins' business. "You're wonderful. Thank you."

I must have had a little too much of the champagne Alan splurged on, because I'd never have gushed that way to my boss otherwise. Virginia laughs and hugs me again.

When Ben and I finally reach my house, all is quiet. Ben halts his truck in my driveway, and we sit still for a time, reveling in the silence.

"Want me to go?" Ben asks softly. "It's been a big night. I understand if you're overwhelmed—"

I haul myself across the seat and crush his lips to mine. "Stay," I murmur. His answering smile is all I need.

We finally go inside, kissing as soon as the door is closed. We kiss in the foyer, the living room, and then down the hall to the bedroom. My aunt smiles from her picture on the mantel, happy for us too.

We kiss in the bedroom, and shed our clothes. Soon we're on my bed, wrapped in each other, bathed in moonlight.

"Sure you don't want me to go home?" Ben jokes as he slides inside me, my world opening and flooding me with euphoria.

"No." I groan the word, and hold him close. "Please stay. Forever ..."

"I can do that."

Our words drift away—no more need for speech.

I'm with Ben, the man I love. We come together in a perfect dance, two partners well matched as we float away on love, happiness, and an effervescent wave of pleasure.

Epilogue

One month later
Austin

I KNOW she'll be here. I'm bracing for it, but when I walk into the church for Abby and Zach's wedding rehearsal and see the beautiful woman in the tight blue dress, my tongue gets stuck in my throat.

Brooke Marsh. My ex.

The sheath dress shows off her legs, bare for the June heat. Her arms, which used to wrap languidly around me, are likewise bare. Her black hair is long and sleek, hanging in a satin swath halfway down her back, complementing her dark eyes.

Brooke greets me cordially, even as a tightening around her mouth betrays her tension. What we had together was a long time ago, and we've both moved on. Right?

Sure.

I'm a groomsman for Zach, and Brooke is a bridesmaid for Abby. Fortunately we aren't slated to walk out together after the ceremony—my brother and soon-to-be sis-in-law are more shrewd than that. No trying to slyly pair us up—I'll be escorting Cheri, another of Abby's friends.

The rehearsal begins soon after I arrive, the minister taking us through the process. Mom looks like she wants to cry, but bears up. She's had Ryan married off, now Zach, and in the fall, it'll be Ben. The youngest son, me, is the only one still unattached.

We go to dinner afterward at a nearby restaurant. Mom won't let me skip it, so I show up. Besides, I want to support Zach.

I'm gallant to Abby's friend Cheri, who I can tell is not interested in me other than as her friend's new brother-in-law. Brooke, paired up with Zach's friend Nate, laughs, flicking back her smooth hair in the way I remember so well. A little pain starts in my chest, and it's not from the stuffed jalapeños.

I manage to avoid being one-on-one with Brooke until the dinner is breaking up. The restaurant has a courtyard with a fountain, a cool space after the sun goes down. I step out to catch my breath, believing the courtyard empty.

I hear a rustle, and there's Brooke, rising hastily from an iron bench where she's been sitting under a spread of oleander. The heavy scent from the blossoms blends with the night.

We face each other. Brooke is as beautiful as I

remember. I try to recall the bad times with her, the arguments, the wild words, the raw impatience.

But all I can think of is how hot we'd been together.

"Hey," I say, as though she's a casual acquaintance I haven't seen since the last family wedding.

Brooke's brows draw down, as though she's annoyed I spoke first. "Hey."

"So. Um." I cast around for something to say. What would I talk about if she were only an acquaintance? "I hear you're running a luxury car business."

A nod. "I'm part owner now."

"Cool." I regard her in true admiration. Brooke has always been smart, capable, astute—and stunning. "I've thought about buying a luxury car, like a Bugatti, but you know ..." I shrug. I make good commission on the sales deals I grab for my parents' business, but they won't make me a billionaire anytime soon.

"Don't be too sure." Brooke speaks nonchalantly, but I see her canny inner saleswoman awakening. "Maserati makes some great entry cars that have a ton of amenities. Or you could go for something like a Spider. Or consider a gently owned car—a few dings on the bumper, and purists shun it, but someone who buys it for the hell of it saves a lot of cash."

"Hmm." I'd thrown out the idea just to make conversation, but I realize that yes, a fantasy car would be fun to own. My brothers will say I'm compensating for my sucky love life, but they can kiss my ass. "Maybe I'll check it out."

Brooke slides her fingers into a minute pocket in

her dress where it curves over her hip. I'd never have guessed the dress had a pocket or that anything could have fit *inside* it.

As I hold my breath, mesmerized by her shapely hip, her fingers come out of the pocket with a card between them.

"Now that I've told you what you can do, don't you dare go to any dealer but mine." Brooke holds out the card. "You think about it, and come see me."

Purely for business. I hear that in her voice. I shrug and reach for the card.

When I clasp it between thumb and forefinger, a spark jumps across the cardboard. I swear.

She doesn't let go. For a moment, we hold the card together. I feel Brooke's grip through the flimsy card, and the pain in my heart expands to full-blown fire.

Our gazes connect. I see in her eyes the flame that once burned between us like the desert sun in the heart of June.

A swallow traces her throat. I let the corner of my mouth twitch into a half smile.

Brooke quickly releases the card. A cool breeze dances across the courtyard, damping our fires.

"All right then." Brooke backs away. "Maybe I'll see you."

"Maybe you will." I put plenty of promise into the words.

I like that she shoots me a glance of trepidation before she turns on her spike heel and hurries back into the restaurant.

I flip over the card, which is a dark blue, almost the same color as her dress. On it is a photo of a red Ferrari, with Brooke leaning casually on its fender. The logo *Paradise Luxury Cars* blazes from the top of the card. Under that is her name: *Brooke Marsh, Owner / Manager.*

"Maybe you will," I whisper to her retreating and beautiful back.

The breeze, cooled by the trickling fountain, carries my words into the night.

———

THANK YOU FOR READING! DON'T MISS AUSTIN and Brooke's story: *Never Say Never,* Book 3 of the McLaughlin Brothers.

About the Author

New York Times bestselling and award-winning author Jennifer Ashley has written more than 100 published novels and novellas in romance, urban fantasy, mystery, and historical fiction under the names Jennifer Ashley, Allyson James, and Ashley Gardner. Jennifer's books have been translated into more than a dozen languages and have earned starred reviews in *Publisher's Weekly* and *Booklist*. When she isn't writing, Jennifer enjoys playing music (guitar, piano, flute), reading, hiking, and building dollhouse miniatures.

More about Jennifer's books can be found at http://www.jenniferashley.com

To keep up to date on her new releases, join her newsletter here:

http://eepurl.com/47kLL